# A STITCH IN CRIME

# A STITCH IN CRIME
## THE TAYLOR QUINN QUILT SHOP MYSTERIES

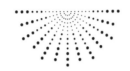

### TESS ROTHERY

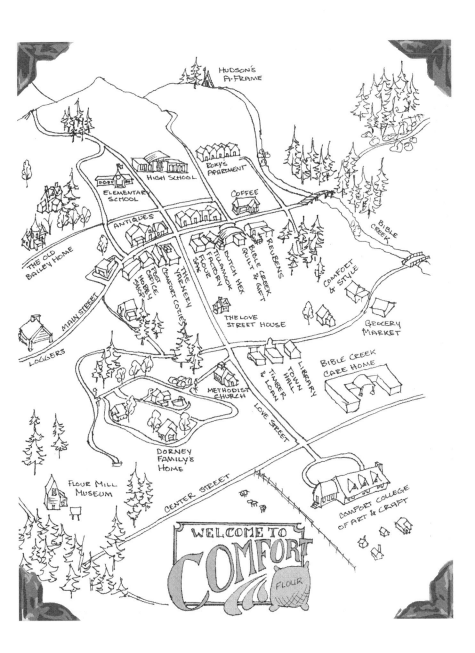

# CHAPTER ONE

Taylor Quinn tucked the folded edge of the crisp new quilting fabric into itself and slid the bolt back into place. The smooth feel of cotton, the vivid colors of the vintage prints that lined the walls, and the slightly dusty aroma of the old building meant one thing to Taylor—home. Taylor's life was rooted here, in the family business, Flour Sax Quilt Shop.

Long ago her Grandpa Ernie had been a tailor specializing in men's bespoke suits. But times had changed, and his beloved wife, Grandma Delma, had turned his storefront business into Comfort, Oregon's first quilt shop. Named for the feed and flour sacks that defined the resourcefulness and style of the depression era, Flour Sax was the seed that had turned Comfort into a quilting destination.

Flour Sax was a lovely place, and it would be hard to say goodbye.

"Lost in the clouds again?" Roxy Lang called Taylor back to earth. Roxy had been working at Flour Sax as long as Taylor could remember. She and Taylor's mom, Laura, were dear friends. Though Roxy had seniority, Laura had put Taylor in charge for the next two weeks. A sort of last hurrah with the family business before Taylor drove away for grad school.

Taylor's mom and baby sister were in California for a bit of a vacation. Belle's dance troupe had been invited to perform in Disneyland and Laura had scrimped and saved for the trip. Laura had made a big deal out of the adventure, but Belle had confided that she was ready to leave tights and tutus behind her. She was almost in middle school, after all. Taylor had pinkie-promised she would not tell their mom. As Taylor was more than a decade older than her eleven-year-old sister, it was sweet to share a secret. But with all the wisdom that comes from being twenty-two, Taylor was sure Belle would never really quit. After all, what else was there to do in a small town like Comfort?

"I am lost in the clouds, I guess." Taylor dusted the cotton bits off the worktable where they cut lengths of fabric for the quilters. "It's strangely nostalgic here without Mom."

"I'd say something about how she'll be home before you know it, but I sort of agree. She's a big presence for such a petite person."

"Too much talk, not enough work," Grandpa Ernie, retired from both tailoring and shop-running, hollered. He might not be on the payroll any longer, but he claimed he had rights to check up on things for "the girls." This had become especially important to him after Grandma Delma, had passed away.

"Sorry, Grandpa! We're closing up as fast as we can. Then maybe dinner at Reuben's Diner?"

"Don't you young people know how to cook?"

Roxy leaned in. "I love it when he considers me one of the kids." Roxy's curly hair was untouched by silver, and her petite frame didn't have an ounce extra on it. It was only when she had her son, Jonah, a quiet grade-schooler, with her that Taylor remembered Roxy wasn't a student at Comfort College of Art and Craft.

"Why don't you both come to mine for supper?" Roxy offered. "I have a chicken dish in the Crock-Pot. Jonah is over at his friend Cooper's tonight, so it will be pretty quiet for me otherwise."

"We'll bring the wine." Grandpa Ernie shuffled into the main room of the shop. He had always been slow of step, taking his time to amble through life, but this time he moved as though he was slowing down. Or his joints weren't what they once were. But his eyes still crinkled when he smiled. Combined with his bushy mustache, he looked like he'd come out of a catalog that specialized in charming grandfathers.

"If you'll close out the register, I'll take out the trash." Taylor pulled a mostly empty bag from the bin under the worktable. "And we'll be almost ready."

Taylor hummed the song her sister was dancing to this weekend as she emptied the many bins that were scattered around the shop. Two weeks running Flour Sax had sounded like a terrific way to spend time before she started grad school for her MBA. She'd adored her time at Comfort College of Art and Craft, but while there, she'd learned she wasn't passionate about creating art. Doing business with crafts people, on the other hand, was something she loved. Flour Sax supported Taylor's family as well as Roxy and Jonah. They even had part-time employees. But Taylor needed to do something else if she wanted a home and family. Maybe in twenty or thirty years when her mom retired, she'd come back. Until then, she had to find her own way. She was keen to try her hand at something bigger, like the corporate office of Craft Warehouse, or Joann Fabric.

"Lost again, Taylor? You've been standing with your hand to the doorknob for half an hour." Roxy ran a little sweeper over the rose-colored indoor-outdoor carpet.

"Only half a minute, surely." Taylor laughed as she stepped into the alley behind the shop, where the dumpsters were kept.

The early summer sun was just starting to set, and the air had cooled. A car drove down Love Street toward the college, and she glanced up to see who it was. It passed too quickly, but she thought it was forest green. Isaiah, who manned the front office at the college, drove a Passat that color, so it was probably him.

The dumpsters behind Flour Sax were shared between several businesses, including the Tillamook Cheese Factory outlet. The refuse from the cheese outlet created an environment in the alley that was not conducive to lingering. Nonetheless, a young woman bundled up in a quilt curled against the recycling bin.

A bubble of compassion welled up. You had to be really down on your luck to seek shelter back here. She set her garbage sack down and approached the woman. "Pardon me. Are you okay?"

When she received no reply, she knelt down and gave her shoulder a little shake. The woman looked clean, and the faint aroma of Love's Baby Soft seemed to come from her gently worn quilt. "Are you okay?" Taylor repeated the question as she patted the woman.

This time, the lady's head tilted to the left, revealing a large, abraded bruise on her forehead. Taylor's heart leapt to attention. She nudged the stranger lightly, hoping to see her eyes open. The woman responded to her touch with a flinch. Whoever she was, she was still alive.

If the woman was alive, she could be helped. That was all that mattered right now. Taylor patted her pockets, but she'd left her phone in the shop. She needed an ambulance, but she didn't want to leave the girl alone. She gave her shoulder a third gentle nudge, but though the woman groaned lightly, she didn't rouse.

"You forgot this one." The gruff voice of Grandpa Ernie interrupted the quiet. He held out a white plastic garbage sack. "Who's that there?" He lowered his bushy eyebrows and stared at Taylor and the lady on the ground.

"I don't know, but we need an ambulance. Can you call?"

"Sure thing. Don't move her case'n she's hurt."

Taylor sat on the asphalt next to the stranger. The woman was young—around about Taylor's age. The quilt she was wrapped in had seen better days, but it was clean. The dusty-blue-and-rose colors of the fabric reminded Taylor of the quilt in her best friend

Maddie's living room. A color story distinctive of the 1980s. She drew her finger along the one-inch border. Though worn and faded, the border had been oversewn with a line of flowers a basic machine could produce, to reinforce the weak areas. The quilt pattern alternated between fussy cut squares of illustrated geese— also very 1980s—and a variation of a block called Courthouse Steps.

While the quilt was nothing to enter in a fair, Taylor liked it. It had been loved and used and cared for, and it was the only thing comforting the injured woman.

FOLKS not from Comfort might have looked askance at the converted van that served as their emergency medical response, but the sight of it turning into the alley was almost miraculous to Taylor.

Adam Reuben, a tall, dark-haired man about ten years older than Taylor, stepped out.

She told him the short story of how she'd found the unconscious lady and watched in admiration as he took her vitals and helped her onto the cot.

"You don't have any idea who she is?" he asked one more time.

"I've never seen her before. But here." Taylor pulled a Flour Sax card from her pocket. "If she needs anything, she can always call me."

Adam accepted it. "You sure? You don't even know her."

Taylor nodded. She was sure. If this girl was a stranger to Taylor, who had at least a passing acquaintance with most of the town, and also a stranger to Adam Reuben, who was a member of one of the largest families here, then she really didn't have anyone else to help her. The ambulance would carry her to the nearest hospital, in a larger town about an hour away. Taylor might not hear from this girl again, but if she did, she was happy to help.

❧

THE NEXT AFTERNOON'S rain put all thoughts of the injured woman from Taylor's mind. The water fell from the sky in sheets. No one was shopping, and fat drips from the ceiling above the window landed on the antique Singer displayed in the front window.

Taylor was hauling the machine toward the center of the shop when the store's phone rang for the first time that day.

Grandpa Ernie answered it and hollered her over.

"Coming." Taylor swiped water off the surface of the sewing table. Her mother wouldn't love it if the wood was damaged while she was away.

"Flour Sax Quilts, this is Taylor Quinn. How can I help you?"

"Taylor?" The caller was an unfamiliar female with an alto voice that sounded as though she might be a wonderful singer.

"This is she." Taylor's eye was on the front door. The rain had turned the midmorning to a steely gray she usually associated with midwinter.

"Um, I... I don't know who I am."

"Pardon?" Taylor's attention was back on the phone call.

"The nurse said you gave me this card when the ambulance brought me to the hospital. They say I have amnesia. I mean, I guess I do, since I don't know who I am. I talked to a police officer, and he gave me your card." She paused, and the quiet seemed to drag on. "I don't know what to do now."

"I see." Taylor rubbed the cuff of her sweater between two fingers. The acrylic yarn had lost its loft years ago, but Grandma Delma had knit the cardigan for her, and she loved it.

"What do the doctors or police advise?"

"They took my picture and my fingerprints. They're starting a hunt to figure out who I am. They said I can stay in the Motel 6 near the station, and they gave me a prepaid Visa gift card. I have a concussion, but I can leave whenever."

"That's great." Taylor tried to sound cheerful, but the story was pretty pathetic, and the woman sounded demoralized. "Text me from your room when you're check in. I can take you to Walmart so you can pick up necessities." Taylor gave her cell phone number to the mystery woman.

"That is so kind. Thank you." She cleared her throat. "I was just wondering… Have you ever seen me before?"

TAYLOR THOUGHT about that question for hours. The pain in the woman's voice as she asked it, the disappointment when Taylor had to say no. At least she didn't think so, but many people came and went during tourist season in Comfort. The nearby Tulip Festival in spring brought people to the area, and they often stopped by for a quick bite and some shopping. Flour Sax and the three other quilt shops in town ran almost constant quilt sales and events. Comfort had worked hard to develop a reputation among quilters that rivaled Sisters in Central Oregon. Guest lecturers came to the College of Art and Craft. Students came and went, too. Comfort was a small town, and yet they had any number of strangers come through. And yet, she would almost swear she'd never seen the woman before.

Taylor was a moment away from closing early when the bells over her door jingled, and a yellow-rain-slicker-clad woman strode in.

"How can you possibly be open in weather like this?" Taylor's paternal grandmother, lovingly called Grandma Quinny by her large passel of grandchildren, slid the hood of her slicker off. She held her arms out, letting the sleeves drip on the front doormat. "I came to see how you were fairing, but I truly hadn't expected to see your lights on. Ernie, what on earth is your granddaughter thinking?" She paused. "Ernie? Ernie?" Her voice resonated through the store.

"I'm just around the corner, Ingrid, not in Canada." Grandpa Ernie came out with his arms crossed and a teasing look of displeasure on his face. The Quinns and the Bakers had remained close friends even after Taylor's father had passed away twelve years earlier.

"What I want to know"—Grandma Quinny kissed Grandpa Ernie on the cheek—"is who the woman was you found behind the shop yesterday."

Grandpa's face melted into a smile.

"I'd like to know that as well." Taylor locked the door. Grandma Quinny was the only person who'd come in all day, and she was right. It was time to close up. "I just spoke to her on the phone. She's got amnesia."

"What is Comfort coming to, that young women get assaulted on Love Street? Ernie, you should have been watching. Can't you see from that old chair of yours?"

A brown corduroy recliner held pride of place in the back of the shop. When not reviewing the books, unboxing product, or chatting up customers, Grandpa Ernie could be found in his chair catching up on the news on a little black-and-white television that sat on top of a mini fridge.

"Yesterday was that accident on the highway up in Seattle. I was glued to the TV," he said with pride. "Mighta been someone we knew."

"In Seattle?" Grandma Quinny chuckled. "When was the last time you left Yamhill County?"

"I don't have to leave, do I? People I know can leave." His eyes twinkled, but there was a worry line between those thick eyebrows of his. "What's new about that girl, Taylor? You spoke to her?"

"Yes, she's who called earlier. She's got amnesia and a concussion. They're putting her up at Motel 6, and I thought I'd take her to Walmart so she could buy some necessities."

"That's a terrible idea. That poor thing cannot stay at a Motel 6 with no one to look after her. I'll come with you, and we'll bring her back to the farm." The Quinns' little patch of land was a strawberry farm, in the loosest possible sense, but its open-door policy to strays was the stuff of legend. "Tell me what to do to help you close this place up, and we'll collect her immediately."

# CHAPTER TWO

G randma Quinny did not look impressed with the Motel 6. "I'd tell you to pack up your bags, but you don't seem to have any."

The stranger wore a light blue T-shirt, jeans, and a pair of white Keds. She clutched the quilt she'd been found with in her arms like a life preserver.

"I can't let you go out like this; that much is true." Grandma Quinny removed her rain slicker, held it to the side, shook the rain drops off, and wrapped it around the girl. "It's terrible out there. We'll buy you something nicer at Target."

"I don't have much on my card." She sent Taylor a pleading look. She looked like she might get swept away in Grandma Quinny's best intentions.

"Think nothing of it. You're my newest tax deduction."

Taylor suspected this wasn't true, but the phrase seemed to comfort the stranger as though it meant she wasn't going to be a burden.

"Come along now, girls. Let's not waste time. There's chicken soup in the Crock-Pot, and Grandpa Quinny has bread in the bread machine. Taylor? Emmy? Are you coming?"

The stranger stopped and stared wide-eyed at Grandma Quinny. "I hate being called Emmy!" Her face broke into a smile. "Oh! That was wonderful. Please, call me Emily. That's my name... and I hate being called Emmy. But how did you think of it?"

GRANDMA QUINNY SMILED as she beeped open her Subaru. "It was an educated guess, my dear. Emily was the top name for girls in America for almost fifteen years. It was immediately replaced by Emma. Odds were one of those was right. If not Emmy, then I'd have tried Sophia, followed by Isabella."

"I know at least three other Emilys." She stopped and stared. "I know at least three other Emilys! This is great! I'm remembering things. I'm Emily D... Emily Donner. Oh gosh, that's fantastic. Thank you so much." Her childlike enthusiasm for remembering her name invigorated all three of them, and they drove off in good spirits.

When they pulled up to Target, Emily burst into another laugh. "Oh! Target, this is good. Okay. I'm Emily Donner, and I used to work at Target. Sometime in my past. I'm sure of it. I have the overwhelming urge to clock in." She gave the store a long, assessing look. "Not this Target though."

"Very good, very good. Let's get you a bit of everything, and see what else you can remember." Grandma Quinny patted Emily gently on the shoulder and strode straight to the store.

"Did the police try to help you remember who you were?" Taylor pulled a cart out of the corral and the women headed toward ladies' underwear.

"A little, I guess, and the doctor. No one tried to guess my name. I'm supposed to go back for a checkup in the morning."

"I'm glad they didn't attempt to keep you at the hospital." Grandma Quinny considered a plastic-wrapped package of Hanes. "You're much better off at Motel 6. At least you can sleep through the night there. But our farm is better. You should stay with us as well, Taylor."

Taylor furrowed her brows. Her grandmother had a way of taking over. She was currently staying in her old home on Love Street. The little house was home to Grandpa Ernie, her mother, and her sister, Belle. With her mom and Belle gone, it had an eerie quietness to it. She thought Grandpa Ernie probably hated it. He was used to a bustling house full of women.

"I should stay close to the shop." The farm was hardly far, but she wanted a reason to stay at home that wouldn't come across as an insult to her grandmother's hospitality.

"You're probably right."

"The doctor said my memory was likely to come back quickly." Emily refolded a striped T-shirt and straightened the stack of matching pajamas. "It's funny that he was so right. I could set this whole display in less than three minutes, but I have no idea why I was in your town."

"What about the quilt?" Taylor bumped into a rack of bathrobes as she tried to maneuver her cart. "Does it bring up any memories?"

"Nothing specific, but it makes me feel sort of… at home? That's the best I can think of. It's homelike, though I'd never pick anything like that for myself." Emily chuckled softly. Her laugh seemed spontaneous and easy, coming after many of her statements, and every bit as resonant and lovely as her speaking voice. And yet it didn't seem normal to be laughing this much.

"Have you had anything to eat today?" There was no line at the Target café.

"I had oatmeal at the hospital."

Retail therapy was something Taylor usually endorsed with a whole heart, but something about the dazed look in Emily's eyes and that laughter, made her think they ought to sit down and have a burger. "Let's pause for a sandwich, Grandma. It's been a long day for Emily."

"You're right. She needs to eat, and we could probably use something as well." She gave Taylor a little wink.

Grandma Quinny handled their food order, requesting three Caesar salads.

The young woman running the café register's name tag said "Megan." Megan had a fresh-faced, makeup-free look, but she also had two bright blue streaks in her dark hair. Taylor glanced at her grandmother, sure the girl was getting a severe but silent critique. Grandma Quinny, however, was smiling kindly and adding items to the order—popcorn, big pretzels, and drinks.

Emily leaned close to Taylor and whispered, "I know her. I mean, I think I do."

"Excellent." She gave Emily's arm a reassuring squeeze. Emily's memory coming back so quickly was a fun combination of relief and thrill. Soon they'd know not only who she was, but what on earth had led to her head injury. "You should say something."

Grandma Quinny paid for the meal and waved away both Taylor's and Emily's cards.

Emily cleared her throat. Her face had gone pale, and a little sheen was on her forehead as though talking to Megan scared her.

Taylor gave her what she hoped was a reassuring nod.

"Um... hi." Emily gripped her hands together. "Did you, um, ever work at a different Target?"

"Nope." Megan smiled politely and turned to get their food.

"Um, I'm sorry. One more thing." Emily straightened up as though trying to find her courage.

"Yes?" Megan's customer service face was firmly fixed in place.

"You look so familiar. Do we know each other from somewhere else?"

Megan shrugged. "I don't think so."

"It's okay. You probably recognize her from shopping here." Taylor gently led Emily to the table. "Just because she doesn't know you, doesn't mean it's not a real memory."

But as they sat down with their pre-boxed salads and an assortment of snacks, Emily stared at Megan. And as they left the store loaded down with clean underclothes, a new jacket, a few pairs of jeans and shirts, and a simple blue purse, Emily looked haunted.

Taylor had fully intended on sleeping in her bed in the room she used to share with her little sister, but she changed her mind. The almost-moment with Megan had sapped the energy and even the hope from Emily. It seemed like an act of kindness to stick around until she had her feet on the ground.

THE NEXT MORNING, after a breakfast of pancakes and strawberry syrup made with love by Grandma Quinny, and served with a smidge of flirting by Grandpa Quinny, Taylor had to head back to the store.

They would open at eleven, but Taylor needed to check on the damage from the rainstorm. The rose-colored carpet could take a licking, being indoor-outdoor, but that didn't mean everything else in the store had survived the deluge. She was particularly worried about all the wicker baskets full of fat quarters, clearance remnants, and notions her mom had scattered around the shop floor. That and the electricity in the classroom space. Grandpa Ernie had wired that room to accommodate many tables of sewing machines, and Taylor personally doubted he'd consulted any kind of electrician when he'd done it.

"Come along with me," Taylor suggested, as she drew her denim jacket on. "We can talk more and see what else you remember."

Emily was rinsing dishes at the sink. She offered an unenthusiastic okay in reply.

"I think maybe not." Grandma Quinny slid the coffee carafe into the machine. "We'll come by after it opens and see how you're doing. Maybe take lunch together. I'd like to call the police station, give them her name, and see how their search is going. I suspect

Sheriff Rousseau posted her face on the Facebook and left it at that. We can do better."

"Ingrid is good at this." Grandpa Quinny gave his wife a kiss on the cheek as he passed through. "Trust her with your friend."

Grandpa Quinny was right. Grandma had a knack for taking care of people. It left Taylor out of the fun, a bit, but this wasn't about her. "Does that sound good to you, Emily?"

Emily nodded. Her gaze was off in the distance, out the kitchen window.

Emily had been quiet since their trip to Target. She'd only eaten a little dinner and gone to bed early. Taylor was glad she'd stayed near, even though Grandpa Ernie had grumped about it when she'd called him. But despite her best intentions, Emily hadn't seemed to want Taylor's company.

"Call if you figure anything out." Taylor rattled her keys as she waved goodbye. It would be like her grandmother to restore Emily's memory before lunch and deliver her safely to her real home. That would be for the best, of course. So, Taylor stuffed aside the flutter of envy that had arisen. The important thing was for Emily to remember her life, not for Taylor to be the one who helped her do it.

THE SHOP WAS quiet when Taylor made it in, but Roxy was speaking with a young man who was staring at the water stain on the ceiling.

"You remember Hudson East, right?" Roxy asked, as Taylor put away her purse and jacket.

Taylor gave the tall, broad-shouldered, handsome man a good look over. She absolutely remembered him. He'd gone to school with her for her whole life. He was four years younger, though, so she most recently recalled him as the rather tall freshman when she was a senior. He'd had a growth spurt between eighth grade and high school, and all the girls had noticed.

"Hey." Taylor flipped through a stack of mail that had been set next to the register.

"I, uh..." Hudson cleared his throat. "I do a bit of handyman work and was checking to see if any of the buildings on Main Street needed anything after yesterday's storm."

Taylor looked up from the mail. Hudson was almost as handsome as the guy who'd been driving the ambulance. She zipped through the math—he had to be at least one year into college. It wasn't weird for her to flutter a little when she admired him. She had never considered herself man-crazy, but there hadn't been many men at the College of Art and Craft, so she appreciated them when she happened across one.

"I wouldn't even know where to start." Taylor almost fanned herself with the mail but dropped it quickly. It was one thing to appreciate a good-looking man; it was another to act like a fool.

"Hudson's young, but he has experience. He helps out at his aunt's bed-and-breakfast, and didn't you study woodworking in college?"

If Taylor wasn't mistaken, Hudson blushed. "Yeah, but the program wasn't right for me. I'm working with a local builder now. Anyway, I can head upstairs to see about that leak, if you're interested. Otherwise, the shop looks pretty good."

"Thanks. You might as well since you're here." Taylor's smile felt a little too wide, and her voice sounded a dash too girly. Ridiculous.

"I've got time." He plunged both hands into the pockets of his jeans.

"Cool." A phone call interrupted their conversation. Taylor grabbed it. When was the last time she'd said "cool" in reply to anything? "Flour Sax Quilt Shop, this is Taylor speaking."

While she answered questions about their quilt-batting selection, Roxy took Hudson upstairs. There were going to be actual men in her MBA program. She needed to pull herself together, or she'd be a mess for the next two years.

. . .

NOT LONG AFTER she opened the shop for the day, the bell over the door jingled, and Emily stepped in. She was clean and tidy and freshly dressed in the new clothes they'd gotten at Target. Emily had one of those attractive, pleasant faces with strong bone structure. The dark bruising on her forehead and the abrasion that had little scabs were a bleak reminder of her recent trauma.

"Your grandma is wildly generous." Emily leaned her elbows on the register desk as though she wanted the conversation to be private.

"Oppressively generous, is another way to describe that," Taylor said.

"While I appreciate everything she's done for me, I haven't been able to remember anything new today."

"Let me guess." Taylor scooched a basket of thimbles closer to herself and began to stack them by color. It was one of those little mindless tasks that kept her hands busy and made it easier for her to concentrate. "Grandma Quinny hasn't given you two minutes alone to get your thoughts together, but has fed you buckets of the most delicious food ever?"

"I certainly haven't been hungry. And no, I haven't had a minute to myself. I told her I wanted to go out for a walk to see if the town spurred my memory. She offered to come with me, but that hero, your grandpa, said he needed her at home, and then he winked at me."

Taylor had turquoise thimbles on her fingertips and tapped the desktop with them in a happy little rhythm. "Grandpa Quinny is pretty excellent. I'm not sure how any of us could put up with Grandma if he wasn't around."

"I heard that." A gruff voice came from the staircase to the apartment above their store. Grandpa Ernie came down slowly and joined them. "I don't want to hear any disrespect toward that good woman, even if she can be a pill." He had a twinkle in his eye, but Taylor knew he meant it. Ernie Baker had always been big on respecting your elders. "That grandson of Boggy's sure is a smart boy." Grandpa Ernie looked up at the ceiling as he spoke, so Taylor surmised Hudson was the grandson in question.

"I'll tell your mama she has to hire him. That rain made a waterfall straight down from a hole in the roof. It poured through the bedroom wall, then puddled around the light fixture. That's the drip you see there." He nodded at the wet splotch on the ceiling. That window has a problem, too." This time he gestured to the front of the shop. He shook his head and grumped his way back to the utilities closet where he stashed his tools.

"Your grandmother told me everything there is to know about this town. She hoped it would remind me why I'm here. Unfortunately, it didn't. I'm no closer than I was when I woke up at the hospital. She did say quite a bit about the college. I wondered if maybe I'd come to town to go there."

"That could be." Taylor stacked the turquoise thimbles and turned them with her thumb, appreciating the dimpled surface of the hard rubber. "You remember your name and that you used to work at Target. Have you remembered anything else, like maybe who your parents are or where you're from?"

A look of sadness washed over Emily's face. "It's funny, I do. I remember Mom and Dad. I can kind of picture them in my head. But I can't seem to pull up any more details, like their names or phone numbers." Her hand gripped the cheap flip phone they'd picked up at Target the day before. "Even if I could remember, it's not like I could search for them on this. So, I guess I have to wait until the police call me. I'm sure it will be soon. They said they posted on Facebook, and they have my name now. It can't be that hard."

"It should be superfast." Taylor didn't use much social media and didn't have strong opinions on whether it would be a useful way to find Emily's family, but it was clear Emily needed some encouragement. "You said you want to check the college? As soon as Roxy comes back downstairs, I'd be happy to go with you."

"That would be nice." Emily picked up a wheel of beeswax and rolled it over and over in her hand.

"When we found you, did you have anything in your pockets? I know you didn't have your purse on you."

"My pants had fake pockets. The only thing I had was the blanket."

"Quilt," Taylor corrected unconsciously. "Sorry about that. I've grown up around quilters, and they are protective. So much time and money goes into each creation that nobody calls them blankets. But that doesn't matter right now. You had a lovely quilt with you. Maybe that has something to do with why you're in town. Does anything new come to mind when you see it?"

"No. It's just as bad as trying to think of my parents' names. I know when I look at it that I love it. And when I rub my fingers on it, it comforts me. But that's it. I wonder if I made it."

"You couldn't have." Taylor's answer was immediate. The quilt had been cared for, but it was worn thin, and the fabric was long out of style. It couldn't possibly have been made by someone as young as Emily.

Emily's face fell, and she placed the beeswax back in the small basket next to the thimbles.

"But take heart," Taylor said. "We'll go to the college and ask questions."

Footsteps echoed down the stairs as Roxy and Hudson returned.

"He's got an excellent plan." Roxy's voice carried as she came down the stairs. "I'll make sure your mom hires him."

"Fantastic," Taylor agreed. If both Roxy and Grandpa Ernie liked him, she was sold. "I'm glad that's sorted. If you don't mind, I'll take my break now. Emily and I want to go to the college to see if they know why she's in town."

"I was just headed that way," Hudson said. "I want to make sure all the school buildings are doing okay. Their maintenance crew might need an extra pair of hands after that storm."

"Good idea," Roxy said. "Who knows who assaulted poor Emily. I'd rather you two walk with Hudson than head out alone." There was just that twinkle in Roxy's eye that made Taylor think Roxy's real motive had very little to do with their safety.

# CHAPTER THREE

Love Street stretched the entire width of town, from the college on one end to the elementary and high school on the other. As a child, it had measured the whole world. But now, as an adult hunting for answers for Emily Donner, the road was practically nothing.

The walk would have taken minutes, but they were stopped halfway by a blowsy woman with fluffy hair driving a minivan. "Taylor!" She hollered the name as she rolled her window down. "Taylor, Hudson, is that the girl who was assaulted?"

"Hi, Mrs. Dorney." Hudson nodded in greeting.

The woman barked a laugh. "I'd say call me Sissy, but I still have a hard time believing you're all grown-up. I thought you and Tansy would be children forever."

Sissy Dorney. Taylor tilted her head. Sissy's son was a friend of Belle's. She knew Sissy but not to say hi to. Sissy's stepdaughter, Tansy, was younger than Taylor, and all of her other kids were around Belle's age. More importantly, Sissy ran a salon, but Taylor never went to her, so they weren't really on speaking terms.

"Taylor, I wanted to talk to you." Sissy was dressed down in an Adidas warm-up jacket, with her thick, curly hair pulled back in a ponytail. Suddenly Taylor wondered if she'd ever paid up for the last fundraising race her mother had made her sponsor Sissy in. She tucked her hands in her pockets, a little embarrassed that she couldn't recall.

"I can call you later, if you'd like." Taylor wished another car would come sidling along and honk to make Sissy get moving.

"Right now is fine. Hold on, Breadyn, I've got gummy snacks in my purse." The second part of Sissy's statement seemed to be for the whining young person in the back seat. Sissy tossed a large bag behind her and then leaned on the window. "I saw your friend before you found her."

Emily stepped forward. "You saw me? What do you mean?"

"I mean I saw you. You wandered into the alley wrapped up in God knows what kind of blanket."

"Quilt," Taylor muttered.

"You cut across Love Street and sort of meandered back behind Flour Sax. I had a client I needed to get to, so I couldn't stop. Anyway, you had that"—Sissy looked at Taylor and winked—"quilt around you, so I figured you must have been headed to one of the fabric stores."

Taylor did not say *quilt shops,* but she thought it. She also had a dozen questions she wanted to ask Sissy. "Did you see any cars around?"

"Joanne Gregory was coming back from Ruebens, but that was it. It was a quiet morning."

"Any other pedestrians?" Taylor asked.

"No, officer, no *pedestrians* that I saw." Sissy scrunched up her nose in thought. "Wait! That's not true. Phillip was coming up the street, but he was pretty far away."

"Phillip?" Emily said the name quietly. "Is Phillip a redhead?"

"Phil hasn't had any hair for the last twenty years." Sissy revved the engine of her battered minivan. "I can't stand around talking all day, I've got things to do."

Taylor caught Hudson's eye. Sissy had waylaid them, not the other way around.

Hudson shrugged but offered her a little smile.

"May I call you later?" Emily asked in her smooth, low voice.

"Why not?" Sissy held out her hand.

Emily passed her phone over and waited while Sissy input her number.

When they resumed their walk, Emily seemed hung up on the name Phillip. "Are there any other Phillips in your town? Or... are there many redheads? Or perhaps a family with the last name Phillip? A weird coincidence that a man named Phillip would be walking down the street at the same time I was, but the name is really sticking."

"Is your dad's name Phillip, maybe?"

"No..." She stopped. "Ha. No. His name isn't Phillip. That's kind of funny, isn't it? I can tell you with absolute certainty it's not Phillip, but I have no idea what it is. I'm hoping someone on Facebook will recognize my picture and contact my parents, though with the time difference..."

"Time difference?" Hudson frowned. He'd been setting a fast pace toward the school, and seemed impatient, but this stopped him. "What do you mean?"

"If it weren't so awful having no idea what's going on, this would be kind of fun, like a game," Emily said, before explaining herself. "But I am one hundred percent sure my parents are far away right now, and the time difference will mean it's hard for them to contact me."

"Right now?" Taylor agreed this was a fairly fun game, though she regretted whatever nightmare had caused it for Emily. "Do you mean your parents are usually in the same time zone you are?"

"Of course they are. I live with them." She grinned. "I live with them! Oh, that's very good. I live with my parents. Or, lived with, I suppose, since I'm here."

"The next question is whether they are out of town, or you are."

"Both of us, I think," Emily said. "Please don't ask me to explain how I know, but I'm sure that my parents are out of town for a little while. Mark and Stacy."

"Your parents are Mark and Stacy?"

"God, that's a relief." Emily was almost skipping down the street. "Any minute, it will fall into place like those elaborate dominoes. "Thank you, Taylor. Thank you so much."

"I don't feel like I've done much of anything."

"If I were alone at the Motel 6, I'd hardly have someone to talk things through with, and I think the talking is what's doing it."

It had been less than a month since Taylor had graduated from the lauded halls of Comfort College. The homey aroma of floor polish, lemon oil, and Isaiah's musky-herbal scent in the front office enveloped her like a homemade quilt.

"Ladies." Isaiah pulled himself away from his computer. "How can I help you?" Taylor's old friend was dressed in a crisp white button-down shirt with bright gold buttons. She would have bet any amount he was wearing alligator shoes, as well, but his feet were hidden by the impressive antique front desk.

"Hey, Isaiah, I'm sure you heard about what happened at Flour Sax recently."

Isaiah's eyes went wide, and he looked Emily up and down. "Was that you? Poor girl!"

Emily nodded, then told him everything she remembered—both about the incident and about herself. "You don't happen to know if I was supposed to be here at the college for something, do you?"

Isaiah held up one finger and then went back to his computer. "We're closed for the next two weeks. There's nothing on my calendar, and if it's not on my calendar, it doesn't exist."

"What about the fiber-arts instructors? Is there a chance someone's hosting a private class or something along those lines?"

"Nothing anyone told me about." He leaned forward and lowered his voice: "And people tell me everything."

Taylor glanced down the long hall and wondered if Hudson had found who he was looking for.

"Taylor, since you're here, maybe you can help me with a little something."

Taylor flipped her attention back to Isaiah. "Sure."

"One of the students left a project, and for the life of me, I can't remember whose it is. Come back into Morgan's office and see if you recognize it."

"I'll be just a second." Taylor followed Isaiah into the hallowed realm of the administrative offices. He was, she was happy to see, wearing a fantastic pair of shoes.

Once in the office of the vice principal, Isaiah shut the door, and sat on the desk. "How much do you know about this girl?"

"About as much as she knows."

"Be careful. I'm sorry she was assaulted, but what she is describing does not sound like normal amnesia."

Taylor shifted. She'd not had disciplinary action while a student, but this was the room it would have happened in. And despite being the office administrator, Isaiah had an air of authority as he sat on top of that desk, that made her nervous.

She trusted Emily.

Shoot, Grandma Quinny trusted Emily, and Grandma Quinny had excellent instincts.

"She seems pretty sincere in her search for her memory."

Isaiah met her statement with stillness. He was focused just slightly above her head.

"Grandma Quinny believes her."

Isaiah smiled lightly. "Okay, then." He slid off the desk. "But you and Ingrid need to write down everything she says. Keep thorough notes and compare them. If her story shifts over the next few days, be willing to step away. You are good at helping people, Taylor, but you don't have to help everyone."

Taylor's mouth went tight. Emily had been hit on the head and lost her whole memory. Someone was running around, free as a bird, after hurting this girl, and Isaiah was cautioning Taylor to quit helping? That just didn't seem right. "Isaiah, I didn't abandon you when your dog—"

"Stop. I can't." He waved a hand in front of his face.

She understood. Losing his dog to violence had really devastated him, and half the school. Taylor had helped him get to the bottom of what had happened, and she thought she ought to do the same for Emily.

Isaiah was right. Taylor did like to help people in crisis. And whatever the cause, Emily was in a crisis.

"Thank you for caring about me," Taylor finally said. "But Emily needs someone to care about her right now, too."

Isaiah shook his head as he opened the door. "Oh, Taylor, someday this is going to get you in trouble."

She patted his shoulder as she passed. Maybe helping people in crisis would get her in trouble someday, but not this time.

# CHAPTER FOUR

The early summer sun blazed the next morning, and Flour Sax bristled with customers. Though if Taylor wanted to be accurate, no one was shopping. Everyone wanted the juicy story of the mysterious girl who'd been assaulted behind the shop.

Grandpa Ernie held court at the worktable where five women hung on his every word. Taylor couldn't hear clearly, but she recognized "shock," "awe," "strong," "man," and "Laura." She attempted to piece those together as a puzzle. She bet Grandpa Ernie was telling the ladies that Taylor and Roxy were in shock from the event but awed by the presence of a strong man such as himself. As for Laura, Taylor suspected he wished for her competent air of authority. Or maybe he was glad she was far from harm. Either way, Grandpa Ernie liked putting on a show, and the quilters of Comfort ate it up.

Another bundle of women whom Taylor secretly referred to as "The biddies who brunch" were gathered around Roxy, but after a long conversation, they turned and bustled out as one. The shop quieted down as the chatty bunch headed to Ruben's for their weekly gossip and meal. Then, slowly but surely, the store emptied out.

Roxy and Grandpa Ernie remained at the worktable, discussing a delayed fabric order.

While hungrily eating up the gossip, the citizens of Comfort had touched and moved every touchable and movable product in the shop. Tidying up would take Taylor until closing time.

She was bent over picking up a stack of patterns called corn and beans when a loud crash erupted in the family shop. Her heart seemed to burst from her chest, and she dropped to her knees with her arms over her head. She started a slow count to calm her brain, but before she got to four, Roxy ran into the room with Grandpa Ernie right behind her.

"Did you drop a sewing machine through a window?" Roxy asked with a scared laugh.

"Looks like some hoodlum causing trouble." Grandpa Ernie stopped by Taylor, leaned down, and placed his hand on her shoulder.

Taylor slowly unfurled and looked around. The front window had splintered into a million pieces all over the window display and the front of the store. This season's discounted flat folds and several baskets of novelty notions were coated in slivers of glass. The rose-colored indoor-outdoor carpet sparkled with the debris. And in the middle of the mess sat a brick without even so much as a note tied around it.

"That's just inconsiderate." Roxy nudged the brick with her foot.

"Wait!" Taylor waved her hands to keep Roxy from moving anything. "That's evidence. We need to call the police." She tried to catch Grandpa Ernie's eye. She needed that gruff, strong, loving face to give her a sense of security in the middle of this mess.

He was already on the phone and offered her exactly the warm, comforting look she'd hoped for.

"Roxy..." Grandpa Ernie hung up the telephone. "Take her to the diner. Get her something to eat."

"I admire you for wanting to take care of your family," Roxy said with gentleness, "but she's the only witness. The police will want her."

Taylor stood and attempted to put a little steel in her spine. Roxy was right, though Taylor hadn't seen a thing.

BY THE TIME the police arrived, she wished she'd taken up Grandpa Ernie's offer.

"What on earth happened here?" Seconds after the police showed up, Grandma Quinny broke into the scene with her flowered rain jacket billowing behind her like a superhero. Emily stood on the sidewalk, staring through the broken window.

Grandma Quinny pushed her way past two officers who were taking photos of the damage. A young police officer stood behind Grandma Quinny. He was too short to see over her head. He cleared his throat, but it did nothing to remove Grandma from the center of the moment.

"Ingrid Quinn, you go straight home to your husband. This is no place for a lady." Grandpa Ernie stared at her from under his bushy eyebrows.

"This is no time to take the high and mighty with me, sir."

The little police officer stepped around Grandma Quinny and kicked the brick over with his foot. "Well, that's convenient."

Taylor stared at the brick. Thick black letters written with something like a poster marker spelled out "leave Emily alone".

The police left with statements from everyone and took the brick with them.

Grandma Quinny attempted to hustle everyone back to her house, but Grandpa Ernie reminded her he had to stay to board the window up. A quick call discovered that Grandpa Quinny had plenty of spare boards in his barn and would be on his way.

But Taylor's grandmother was undeterred and mother-henned the rest of them right back to her farm, waving to her husband as they passed each other on Bible Creek Road.

After settling everyone around her kitchen table, Grandma Quinny initiated the conversation.

"First, Emily will update you on what we learned at the police station." Grandma Quinny held her hand out to Emily as though passing a microphone.

"Facebook was ridiculously quick to find my parents. I Face-Timed them." Emily's smile had hope in it. "I still don't know why I'm here. I suppose it was just a road trip or something silly. It was nice to hear their voices. They're in Denmark visiting cousins or they would come back right away. But they're sending my brother to town. I didn't tell my parents I'd forgotten I had a brother. I was embarrassed to tell them how much I had actually forgotten." Her finger fluttered to the mulberry-and-indigo bruise that spilled across her forehead. "After my identity was confirmed, the police found my license plate number. I guess I drive a pretty generic gray Toyota. They say they're looking for it, but who knows?"

"I would have assumed someone hit you and stole your car, but the brick through my window makes me reconsider." Taylor sipped her coffee. Grandma Quinny never stinted on her hospitality, and this was the best cup she'd had in ages.

"You're of one mind with the police." Grandma Quinny pushed a tray of scones and strawberry freezer jam closer. "Tell Taylor what your parents said about the quilt."

"They didn't recognize the description." Emily stared at her mug.

"I thought you said looking at the quilt stirred memories?" Taylor took a scone and spread the jam liberally on it.

"I swear I'm telling the truth. The quilt stirs up nostalgia. It might have come from a friend's house, or maybe someone gave it to me recently." She paused and furrowed her brow. "I'd like to find my car."

"You'd better let go of that idea." Grandma Quinny brushed scone crumbs from the strawberry printed tablecloth into her hand. "It's likely been stripped for parts already. What if that quilt came from someone in town?"

"It's too bad the quilter didn't sign her work. That would have answered all of our questions." As much as Taylor cared about Emily and quilts, she was itching to be at Flour Sax with Grandpa Ernie, cleaning up the damage to her mother's life's work. "I need to get back to the shop. If you remember anything about the quilt, let me know."

"Proceed with caution, my dear," Grandma Quinny said. "Someone is trying to keep you from helping."

Taylor hated to admit it, but when she combined the brick with Isaiah's friendly warning, she felt a healthy dose of fear.


BY THE TIME Taylor was back at the shop, the window-boarding-up project was almost complete. Grandpa Quinny and Grandpa Ernie stood on the sidewalk, looking like mirror images of each other. Both stood legs apart, arms crossed, chins up as they assessed their handiwork.

"That's gonna hold," Grandpa Quinny declared.

"Yup," Grandpa Ernie agreed.

"Better close up till this matter gets sorted though."

"Yup."

"Probably best if you and Taylor come stay with us for a while." Grandpa Quinny glanced over at Grandpa Ernie.

"Nope."

Taylor smiled. Grandpa Quinny would never get Grandpa Ernie to abandon ship. He was more likely to sleep in the shop than leave it unattended. He'd raised his little family in the apartment above it, after all, and when they'd moved to a house, it had been as close as he could get.

Taylor was on his side in her heart, but she couldn't ignore the logic of leaving well enough alone. Simply leaving seemed like a good idea, too. A brick through a window was one thing, but the next time the assailant got itchy, it might be a brick to someone's head.

In fact, it had probably been a brick to Emily's head that had caused her amnesia. If so, she was lucky she'd lived. Taylor shivered. What on earth could this girl have gotten herself into? And why had she been wrapped so sweetly in that quilt?

"You'll stay with your old grandpa again, won't you, Taylor?"

Taylor jumped at Grandpa Quinny's words. She hadn't realized she'd been noticed.

"I'm already staying with my old grandpa," she tried to tease. "Someone has to look after him."

"This isn't a time for jokes, young lady." Grandpa Quinny had an uncommonly serious note in his voice. "I would rather you both come to our place. There is security in numbers."

"What do you think, Grandpa Ernie? Should we pop by for dinner? Grandma Quinny is a much better cook than I am."

Grandpa Ernie snorted. "You're not kidding. She's the best. We can eat over there, but don't let her trick us into staying."

"I won't fall for it again."

Grandpa Quinny laughed and patted Taylor's shoulder. "The sooner your grandmother sorts out this Emmy-girl's troubles, the better for all of us."

"Was probably drugs." Grandpa Ernie stepped back from his window to assess it from a distance.

"Bet you're right. Some drug sale gone bad, and a local doesn't want to get caught. Thinks a little vandalism will keep people from catching them."

"I ought to have put that camera up you bought me." Grandpa Ernie sighed. "Could have seen who did it."

"Did the police ask the neighbors? How could someone toss a brick through our window and no one see it?"

"They left that little guy to go up and down the street, but he didn't report back."

"Are either of you going to ask about it?" Taylor nudged.

The two men locked eyes.

"Yup," Grandpa Ernie stated. "We sure are."

Taylor smiled. The brick thrower had scared the wits out of her. But standing outside on a sunny June day with the two best men in the world made everything a little less frightening.

Taylor wandered off, leaving her grandfathers to plan their investigation. She needed air and to think. Perhaps her desire to insert herself into Emily Donner's problems were the result of post-college boredom. No one was grading her work anymore. Maybe she'd developed a need for recognition. She scorned the idea. If she was hungry for more grades, she'd get her fill soon enough.

She found herself walking around town, zigzagging in and out of streets she'd known her entire life. She strolled down Center Street, past the old town hall, a board building with a western façade, where the Comfort Quilt Guild met monthly. She'd been to plenty of those meetings in her life. Though after her sister, Belle, had joined the family, Taylor had been allowed to stay home and babysit.

She ought to have been at Belle's performance at Disneyland. That's what a good sister would've done. Roxy would have managed fine. But the idea set Taylor's nerves on edge. If she had gone with her family, she would have instantly been a child again. Her mother would've had every item of their lives planned right down to which underwear they had to change into every morning, and the snacks they had to keep in their jacket pockets.

Taylor had been so, so happy at college for the last four years. The idea of moving a little farther away for grad school felt like a miracle. Most likely, this was nothing more than the natural progression of life. A college graduate was meant to spread her wings and fly.

Taylor paused at the corner of Center and Yamhill. Someone was watching her. She could feel it in the prickles at the back of her neck. She glanced quickly behind her, but the tree-lined street had too many shadows. Instead, she turned quickly up Yamhill, toward Main.

She hadn't had an attack of paranoia this serious since she'd moved to the dorm. Getting out of the family circle had freed her from the fear the world was going to collapse. She'd never mentioned this to her mom, but she'd been fighting this mental battle for years. Somewhere in the back of her mind she knew it was grief, but her mother's grief had seemed more important. She hadn't wanted to add to her worries, so she kept it to herself and looked over her shoulder. And sometimes, when things got really rough, the Quinn girls would head to the city to shop until they forgot all their troubles.

Taylor stopped in front of the house her best friend Maddie's grandparents lived in. This was just that same paranoia, surely.

Nobody was following her.

Something rustled in the lilac bush on the other side of the fence. Taylor's chest squeezed, and then she ran.

She ran till she crossed Main Street and found herself at the doors to the antique mall. The burst of energy made her lungs burn. She stood in the protection of the entryway, catching her breath. The mall was a big, sprawling building that covered the whole block. It might not be Target, but a girl could do some serious shopping here. And what Taylor needed right now was a serious distraction.

Once in the mall, she forced herself to go slowly and admire the quirky collectibles, abandoned heirlooms, and flotsam and jetsam from days gone by.

She stopped at a booth full to the brim of Pyrex. Grandma Quinny and most of her peers had cleaned out their cupboards over the last couple of years, selling these mixing bowls and sundry pieces at garage sales. And clever, clever Belinda May, who ran the booth, had picked them all up. Now people from Portland came in response to Craigslist ads and paid upwards of forty dollars a bowl. Taylor was admiring a blue-and-white bowl with flat handles and a dainty almost Royal pattern in white etched around it, when heavy footsteps rounded the corner, then stopped behind her. She turned. No one was there.

They were likely digging through the vintage clothing in the previous booth, hidden by the cubical-like walls. Taylor put the bowl down, held her breath, and took two steps backward. The vintage clothing booth was empty, but a dark shadow seemed to move to her left. She spun but was too late.

Taylor walked almost on her toes to make as little noise as possible. She walked sideways, with her back to the booths, scanning the aisle before and behind. The heavy footsteps were in the next aisle over.

She needed with all of her heart to see who that was.

Taylor paused at the end of the aisle and held her breath, attempting a moment of perfect silence.

But when she finally stepped around the corner, the aisle was empty. Instead of facing a suspicious man, she was staring at a pair of vintage throw pillows that exactly matched Emily's goose quilt.

She stared at the pillows, comparing the patchwork with what she remembered of the quilt, but it was the same. The same blocks, the same fussy cut geese. The same dusty-rose-and-country-blue color scheme.

It seemed as though she owed her paranoia a big fat thank-you. And a thank-you to whoever was thumping around the store with such loud shoes. She wouldn't have seen these if she hadn't been out of her mind with illogical fear. She grabbed the pillows and ran to the register where she paid for them as quickly as she could. A large man with work boots on was admiring a tableful of woodworking planes. He'd probably been the loud walker.

The booth ticket was Cradle-to-Grave, run by Diana Reuben, a member of the influential and huge Reuben family.

Diana Reuben sold insurance from a little office at the back of her house. Taylor ran straight to her house.

TESS ROTHERY

Diana was just sitting down to supper and invited Taylor to join her for some tuna fish and potato chips.

"Where did you find these?" Taylor threw the pillows on the table.

"Aren't those so cute?" Diana took a healthy bite of her sandwich, which crunched with potato chips. She chewed thoughtfully while looking at them. Eventually she swallowed and turned the pillows front to back.

"Adorable, but where did they come from?" Taylor put on her Flour Sax voice. If she pretended Diana was a customer, she could keep her impatience hidden.

"I got those from a garage sale at... Do you know that cute farmhouse on Blain Road, way back toward the hills? Almost to Moon Creek?"

"Do you know the address? Plenty of farmhouses on Blaine Road."

"Sorry, I didn't think this was a criminal investigation." Diana took a sip of ice water. "Wait, is this a criminal investigation? Is this about that girl?"

"Yes. These match her quilt. I have to know where you found them."

Diana's chip bag rustled as she poured more onto her plate. "So, the house is just north of Moon Creek. It's a big, old place. Probably the oldest one in that area. The family who built it..."

"I don't care who built it. Who lives there now?"

"The house's backstory is interesting, and you never know what might help your friend."

"I am certain it wouldn't help. Seriously. Just... the names of the owners, or the address. Something concrete is all I ask. The history of the house isn't a bit important."

Diana narrowed her eyes. "Some people would disagree."

"Okay, who built the house?" Taylor did her best to slow her breathing down. She stroked the worn cotton of the pillow with just her fingertips. The bumpy, quilted texture soothed her jangled nerves. She had not been able to keep her store-face on, to her shame.

"Well, I don't remember. I wish I did. Hold on. Let me call my mom…"

Taylor squeezed the pillow in a fist. "Please…. the address…"

Diana held up two hands in surrender. "Fine. The family that lives there now bought it earlier this year. They've been fixing it up. I've heard they want to turn it into some kind of bed-and-breakfast."

"Honestly, all I want is the address. Or some landmarks or something."

"Just a second." Diana got up and scrounged around her kitchen. "I've got paper here somewhere. Anyway, the owners are a youngish couple. Not forty yet. I don't think they have kids. Actually, I don't think they want to have a bed-and-breakfast. I'm pretty sure they said they want a retreat center. I got to tour the house. I found the pillows inside. I begged for them. There was a quilt, too, but the antique mall is filled with vintage quilts no one wants. The pillows were different and cute. I thought they would look great on that settee I have in the booth, you know."

Taylor had not noticed the settee. She had not noticed if the pillows were adorable. She'd only noticed it was the exact same fabric and pattern as the quilt.

She suspected she was going to have to drive down Blaine Road, knocking on the door of every farmhouse with a porch. "Is there anything else at all that might help me recognize this house?"

Diana shoved a drawer shut. "Sure! It has a new roof, and a big front porch, plus, it's the one with the funny mailbox."

Taylor waited. She couldn't say it was patiently.

"You know the one. It's sitting on top of a tree trunk that's been carved to look like Big Foot."

Taylor exhaled in relief. She knew exactly the house. Her instinct was to drive immediately to this farmhouse-cum-retreat-center or whatever it was supposed to be. If the people running that house had assaulted Emily and put a brick through Taylor's window, then perhaps she shouldn't rush over.

She played the pros and cons on her way back to Flour Sax. The element of surprise had value, at least according to cop shows. The adrenaline from the discovery made her brave, which seemed a pro, but then again, caution seemed a positive as well. At least when dealing with potentially violent people.

She had come to no conclusion by the time she was back at Flour Sax, so she let herself in and helped herself to a granola bar from the stash of snacks. Once she'd gotten comfy in Grandpa Ernie's recliner, she pulled out her phone only to discover it had been dead for who knows how long.

With a grunt, she pulled herself out of her cozy nest and found a phone charger. Once life had been restored, she found she'd missed a call from her mom.

Her mom, the dear woman, was in a panic. She'd heard the whole story, up to the brick through the window, from Grandma Quinny. "Belle is safe here with the dance team. They've got plenty of chaperones. The dance instructor said she'd take care of her. I can come immediately. I can catch the next flight. Call me back. I don't like you being there alone."

Taylor texted immediately that she was fine and safe. She was far from alone. Between Grandpa Ernie and the Quinns, she had more than enough support. Heck, she bet if she called that Hudson kid, he'd jump at the chance to take care of her. The thought made her grin. Cute kid, Hudson. But she didn't need him, or her mommy to take care of her right now.

That said, if she were to approach the old farmhouse, Grandma Quinny might be the perfect partner.

A quick phone call found Grandma Quinny in complete agreement. In fact, she didn't think Taylor needed to come along.

But she did insist they wait till the next day.

# CHAPTER FIVE

B right and early the next morning, Taylor and her elegant if forceful grandmother were standing on the front porch of a carefully remodeled farmhouse just north of Moon Creek.

A huge hulk of a man answered the door as soon as they rang the bell. He stood at least a foot taller than Taylor and had the broadest pair of shoulders she'd ever seen. In her imagination, her father had been as broad, but she'd been young when he died. This man had Viking proportions and the coloring to go with it, with pale eyebrows, invisible eyelashes, icy-blue eyes, and a bristling blond beard.

"What?"

Grandma Quinny squared her shoulders and tilted her chin up. "We are looking into the case of a young woman who was recently assaulted in Comfort."

The Viking stared with a stony face.

"We have reason to believe she was a guest of yours."

He shook his head.

"Is someone home we could speak to?" Taylor inched forward. If she could get her toe just over the threshold, she could keep the door open. She wasn't sure what had inspired the move, but she liked it. She felt empowered.

"Lonnie!" the man bellowed without even turning his head. A scurry of footsteps sounded in the background, and a woman who looked so much like the man, she could have been his sister, suddenly appeared. Her icy-blonde hair was slicked back into a tight ponytail, giving her an almost bald look. Her eyelashes had been coated in thick mascara, but her eyebrows were almost invisible.

"Hi!" Taylor jumped in before her grandma could. "So, the other day I came across an injured woman. I think she might have come to your garage sale, or maybe stayed at your place."

"I heard about that girl." Lonnie's eyebrows pulled together in thought. "Tons of people came to the sale, but we haven't had any guests."

"When my granddaughter found her, she was wrapped in your quilt."

"The pretty pink-and-blue quilt with the geese," Taylor interjected.

"I wondered what happened to that. Klaus, I've been asking for that for days, haven't I?" Lonnie punched Klaus's shoulder.

Klaus shrugged and then crossed his arms.

"So, um, you may have sold the quilt at the garage sale, then? There was no chance the girl was, like, a friend or something? Someone who'd wandered off with the quilt?" Taylor's heart sped up. There was no way these two were going to admit to assault, though both of them looked like they could knock a girl to the ground with a fingertip.

"Klaus?" Lonnie turned to him, looking like a thunderstorm. "Did you give away *my quilt?*"

"We had an epic garage sale, Lonnie. Even you said it was a success. Just... let it go." Klaus reached for the doorknob. "Sorry we couldn't help." He loomed in the doorway, as though he could move them off his porch with energy alone.

Taylor wasn't done yet. Klaus knew something. They were getting somewhere, and she was fired up. She lunged forward. At the same moment, Klaus thrust the door shut.

Taylor got the edge of the solid walnut door full in the face as it cracked straight across her nose.

The pain was blinding, like a fiery knife. Tears sprang to her eyes, and she was fairly sure snot and blood poured from her nose.

There was some kind of kerfuffle. She couldn't follow the movements, what with the screaming pain in her brain and her eyes pinched shut. But there were hands on her shoulders and then hands pulling her to her feet and Grandma Quinny's voice saying, "Call nine-one-one; what's wrong with you?"

"I can't see," Taylor responded to her grandma's request.

And then her grandma's hand—she could tell it was hers this time—patted her shoulder. "Of course you can't. I'm talking to these people. The people who just assaulted you."

Seconds later, Taylor had an ice pack to her nose and was being seated in a hard, straight-backed chair. She was panting for breath, which felt absurd, but the pain, it was a lot. That said, an ambulance seemed like overkill. Surely her grandmother could have driven her to the urgent care for stitches. While they waited for the EMT, Grandma Quinny got down to business.

"So, about your retreat center."

"Small-town gossip," Lonnie responded. "During the garage sale, I told people about my dreams for the future. I'm sure word spread, but it's far from reality yet."

"But you had a garage sale, and Klaus sold your quilt and pillows."

"The pillows, too? Geez, Klaus! What's your problem?"

"No problem. What did you want with those, anyway?"

"They were mine. I made them. What other reason do I need? I've been asking you about that quilt for days. Were you ever going to tell me the truth?"

"I didn't know it wasn't for sale." Klaus's voice rose in anger, which Taylor suspected was the way some men acted when they felt guilty. "The sale was almost over, and some girl came in looking for stuff for her new apartment. She liked the quilt. Said it reminded her of being a kid or something like that. So, I sold it to her for five dollars. Sorry."

"Jesus in heaven, Klaus. It was completely irreplaceable. I made it in middle school home ec."

"It looked like it."

"You are such an ass."

This didn't feel like it was furthering her cause, but the idea of making a sound made Taylor's stomach flip. The pain was just too much.

"Can you describe the girl who purchased it?" Grandma Quinny asked Klaus.

"She was young, not very tall, kinda skinny and kinda dark. I think she wore a hat."

This wasn't much help since anyone would be dark compared to these two, and anyone was short, for that matter.

Unfortunately, the ambulance arrived before they could get further details from him. That handsome Adam Reubens popped Taylor inside without so much as a friendly hello and drove her to the emergency room.

They stitched her up with something like super glue and butterfly bandages and explained that face wounds always bleed a lot. On the way home, Grandma Quinny said the ambulance ride was worth the cost because of what they learned. Perhaps the effect of the hospital-grade aspirin was at work, but Taylor didn't think Grandma Quinny was right. All they knew was that someone in a hat bought the quilt at a garage sale. They were hardly any closer to learning who had knocked Emily in the head.

# CHAPTER SIX

Grandma Quinny had once again gathered the family together at her farm. Even Grandpa Ernie was at the table. She served hot bowls of leftover chicken noodle soup and more of Grandpa Quinny's fresh bread for lunch. Taylor took careful sips of the broth. Though not broken, her nose was swollen and bruised. Breathing wasn't easy, so neither was eating.

"Your grandma was really nice and let me borrow her computer." Emily spread butter on a thick slice of white bread. "I've chatted with my parents. They suggested they get me an airline ticket to join them in Denmark, but that seemed a bit extreme."

"Not to me," Grandpa Ernie said with a huff. "If you were my kid, I wouldn't want you out of my sight right now."

"Isn't your brother coming to town?" Taylor asked, though it sounded more like "Isn'd your brodder coming do down?"

"Yeah, he texted my burner phone. He said he'll be here tomorrow. I gave him this address. I hope that's okay."

Grandpa Ernie laughed. "I think Ingrid would be right angry if you hadn't. If you hadn't noticed, this strawberry farm doubles as a hostel."

"Oh, Ernie." Grandma Quinny waved away his statement. "But I

45

am very glad you did. It is better to have you together, in my opinion."

Emily fiddled with her phone. "I appreciate it. You've all made me feel like family."

"I think you bought your quilt at a garage sale." Taylor figured her non sequitur could be blamed on her injury. No one would expect her to make sense in her condition. "I found matching pillows at the antique store and tracked down where they'd come from. Does the idea of a garage sale ring any bells?"

Emily scrunched her face. "No, not really."

"The guy who was running the garage sale said the girl who bought it was shopping for her new apartment." Taylor pictured big, burly Klaus. He hadn't wanted to say anything about the quilt or the transaction. One quick blow from his fist could have given Emily a vicious concussion. That said, he'd have to be an idiot to leave her with his wife's quilt. The quilt was too easy to tie it back to him.

"Apartment..." Emily mused on the word. "Is there an old apartment building somewhere here in town? Like, made of brick maybe?"

"Yes." Taylor's heart lightened. They deserved this breakthrough. "Right near the high school. It's the only apartment building in Comfort."

"I can picture a brick building and a really cute, little one-bedroom apartment. I wouldn't swear it was mine, but it sounds familiar. Let's check it out."

"You'll go nowhere till you've finished your soup," Grandma Quinny chastised.

Taylor dearly wanted to lay her head down and not open her eyes until tomorrow, but she nodded. Right after soup, they needed to go see this apartment building.

. . .

THE BUILDING MANAGER was an older woman with a sleek steel-colored bob, large silver-hoop earrings, and an expensive-looking pair of skinny jeans. She stood under the awning of the door to the apartment office holding a heavy metal ring that jangled with keys. "Ingrid! Good to see you." She smiled brightly at Grandma Quinny.

"And you." Grandma Quinny was all business but managed a genuine smile. "Taylor, you know Judy, I'm sure. Her son, Evan, is around your age."

"Good evening." Taylor did not correct her grandmother, though Evan was at least as old as Grandma's youngest son, Sean.

Judy tilted her head. "What happened to you, kiddo? You look awful."

"I ran into a door." Taylor shrugged.

Judy's eyes went wide—the classic cover for domestic abuse hadn't passed her notice.

"The door ran into her, Judy. But that's not why we came. Do you happen to know our friend Emily Donner? She was recently assaulted and found behind Flour Sax." Grandma Quinny pushed Emily forward.

"Oh, Emily, aren't you two just a pair!" Judy held her arms open as though in invitation for a hug. "I'd heard someone was assaulted, and I just had a terrible feeling it was you. You never came back after you dropped your things off."

Emily accepted the big hug. "So, I did rent a place here?"

"Oh goodness, I'd heard about the amnesia. Yes, darling. You rented a one-bedroom. You have a three-month lease, paid the first month in full, plus the cleaning fee, and you moved in with almost nothing for furniture. I was worried for you, but you said you were going to hit up some garage sales and how your car was small so you hadn't wanted to drive too much down with you. Do you have your keys?"

"No. No keys. No wallet. Nothing but a quilt that apparently I did get at a garage sale."

Judy looked around as though she expected them to have the

quilt. "Well, never mind that. I recognize you just fine, and I have a key." She jangled her ring. "I also have a copy of your ID if you'd like it."

"Thank you, that would be nice. It would probably help."

"After we get you settled back in your apartment, I'll run down to the office and make photocopies for you. Come on now, let's get upstairs."

Roxy Lang and her son, Jonah, lived in one of the apartments in this building, it wasn't a large building, but apparently it was large enough that she hadn't recognized her new neighbor.

The apartment was small, and the only furniture were two plastic folding chairs, and a twin-sized air mattress.

"Do you see what I mean?" Judy, the manager, asked. "This and a suitcase full of clothing. I could hardly believe it."

"But my suitcase full of stuff must be here still!" Emily popped open the closet door in the bedroom and sighed with relief. I have never been so happy in my life."

"I'm just glad to have you back safe." Judy glanced at her watch. "Let me get that photocopy of your license. I hope your first night here will be a peaceful one."

"Don't even think about it," Grandma Quinny stated after Judy had left. "Until we know what happened, you are much safer with me." There was a hint of jealousy in her tone that made Taylor smile. Judy seemed warmhearted and like she'd adore mothering the poor, lost Emily.

"But does this make you remember anything?" Taylor sat on the folding chair and rested her head in her hand.

"No." Emily looked up and around. "The building is right. The apartment is right. This is an adorable place. The kitchen is vintagey, and all the trim work is kind of fancy."

The apartment was lovely with wide windows and old-fashioned baseboards and window trim coated in many layers of glossy white paint.

"You were going to rent it for three months… so June, July, and August. It sounds like you had summer plans."

Emily shifted from foot to foot. "What kind of summer plans? That's the question, isn't it?"

THE NEXT MORNING Taylor was only a little better. Tylenol took the edge off her headache, but the dull pain that remained was constant. She had neither the product nor the skill to cover the dark black eye she'd developed from the bruising, so she looked as poorly as she felt.

Roxy and Grandpa Ernie had cleaned Flour Sax the day before, but Taylor was itching to check it out.

Flour Sax didn't look as bad as Taylor had feared, but it didn't look great. Despite both the leaking ceiling and the shattered glass, the carpet had cleaned up just fine. The boarded-up window cast the front of the shop in darkness. The window display was bare. The emptiness gave Taylor a shivery, haunted feeling. She'd removed the old Singer, and everything else had been swept away with the window debris.

The window display had been her favorite part of the store when she was little. Grandma Delma used to let her sit at the antique machine and pretend to sew. One particularly delightful year, just after kindergarten, the display had been filled with all sizes of quilted teddy bears. They were samples made from a pattern that the shop was pushing hard. Taylor and her best friend, Maddie, had spent countless hours playing teddy bear in that window. Grandpa Ernie said the two girls were their best advertising ever. They had quickly sold out of the pattern in the recommended fabrics. Everyone at Comfort Elementary got teddy bears that Christmas.

Taylor itched to fill that empty space, even though the window would be blocked for a while. She pulled two armless side chairs upholstered in linen fabric, covered in a pseudo-French script, into the window.

Then she made what looked sort of like a coffee table by stacking bolts of cotton. She created an earth-tone hombre effect with polka dots and plaid, a sort of quilters woodgrain. She rummaged through the store till she found pieces that could stand in for a tea set. A miniature iron for the teapot, two large pincushions in lieu of teacups, and little rectangular patterns as plates. She was just scrounging around in a bin full of notions to see if she could come up with petit fours, when the phone rang.

"Flour Sax Quilt Shop. This is Taylor speaking." Taylor made a note to mention next time that they were closed for repairs. The last thing she needed was people calling from outside the front door just to make sure they were open and then being mad when she wouldn't let them in. She looked around. She could let them in. But she didn't want to. The shop felt sort of sacred and wounded. And she wanted to protect it from outsiders.

"Taylor, I just had a most interesting conversation with one of my clients." It was the Dorney lady, Sissy.

"I'm guessing this is about Emily." Taylor hitched herself up onto the counter and sat cross-legged, another thing she'd been allowed to do as a little girl.

"Of course it is. It's not like Belle's there, is she?"

Taylor thought for a moment. Yes, it was true. The only other thing Sissy would have called the shop about would be Belle, and Sissy's kid... Cooper? Connor? Taylor never could remember.

"Are you going to ask me about it?"

Taylor was tempted to say no. Being forced to ask for the information annoyed her. Especially as this woman was dying to talk.

"Well?" Sissy nudged.

"What did you learn?"

"A young lady was just in getting her hair done. I've been giving her cute, colorful streaks for a few years, but she wanted to go all-over blonde. I wouldn't do it. It is so hard to get dark hair bleached all the way down the way she wanted it. So damaging, too. And she's one with really nice hair, naturally thick and glossy. There are just some things I have to refuse, you know?"

"Sounds like good advice." Taylor twirled the phone cord between two fingers.

"Well, anyway, this girl was sitting in my chair, and she asked me if I knew anything at all about concussions."

"Because you work with heads?" Taylor stifled a snicker. She knew people turned to stylists for all sorts of reasons, but this one seemed a stretch.

"I assume it's because I have a son, and boys are always hitting their heads." Sissy spoke slowly as though Taylor were dim. This seemed fair since Taylor had literally been laughing at her.

"What did you tell her?"

"I played along. Because this was, as you noticed, a really odd question. I told her it depended on the severity and then asked her for more information. As in, was she wondering how long it would hurt. She very specifically wanted to find out how long amnesia caused by a concussion might last."

"I suppose lots of people in town are wondering the same thing. People do seem interested in our poor friend." Taylor pulled the coiled phone cord till it was straight, and let it snap back into place while she considered this. Emily had been to a garage sale and had rented an apartment. Yet when word spread that a stranger had been assaulted, none of the people who'd seen her came forward to see how she was. Judy, the apartment manager, was a particular worry. Sure, she'd seemed nothing but loving when they met her, but she hadn't even checked to see if the injured person was her renter. This struck Taylor as more than a little suspicious. "Then again…"

"Then again? I'm glad you're questioning your premise. Because as far as I can tell, not nearly enough people are talking about this. When Cooper's friend Dayton got in that skiing accident, broke both arms, and had a concussion, people talked about it for months. I had clients whispering that they wanted to turn Dayton's parents in on suspected child abuse. But the poor child had fallen head over skis, and these things happen. I think for someone who is practically paid to gossip, I have been hearing far too little about your friend."

"Why do you think that is?" Taylor asked.

"Probably because she's not one of us. And she's a pretty, young girl who is apparently single."

"You'd think those would qualify as great subjects for gossip." In fact, it was exactly the kind of thing she and the other students at the college would've been gossiping about if school had still been in session.

"There's a lot of single men in this town, Taylor. Or there would be if they didn't all move away as soon as they graduated high school."

"So, you'd think a pretty, young, single lady moving to town would make people want her to stay, yes?"

"Nobody wants their son to fall in love with someone from out of town. When that happens, you never get the boy back."

Taylor considered this.

It was probably true. She personally had no reason to expect she'd move back to Comfort in the future. There weren't many jobs for someone with a bachelor's degree in fiber arts and a future MBA. While she supposed she could fall in love with someone from Comfort as easily as anyone else, she certainly hadn't yet, and she'd had plenty of time.

"So, you think no one is talking about her because no one wants her here?"

"Exactly. Which brings us back to the girl who was getting her color done. She wanted to talk about it."

"You say she has dark hair?"

"Yes, I gave her a deep-conditioning treatment and a bit of a cut. Touched up her color—went from a sort of aqua to a really pretty cobalt. It suits her."

"Would you say she's particularly small?"

"What are you getting at?" Sissy asked "It's Lindsay from Cuppa Joe's, if you're wondering. She's about your age, I think."

Taylor wasn't sure how to take that. Lindsay was almost a decade older than her.

"I talked to someone who mentioned..." Taylor hesitated. She wasn't sure she wanted to tell Sissy about the quilt. In fact, she absolutely did not. "Never mind. I guess I was just being nosy."

Sissy scoffed. "Aren't we all? Well, now you know Lindsay was curious about amnesia. You might look into that."

"You're right. I just might." Taylor ended the call, glad for a little bit of information but not sorry that Sissy wasn't one of the people she had to deal with on a daily basis.

Taylor stayed where she was but adjusted her feet so she was sitting in the lotus position as she learned in yoga. She reached up and pressed her hands together, then drew in a deep breath and held it. Peace washed over her as her nerves calmed down. She didn't do nearly enough yoga, but when she did, it helped. It wasn't as good as shopping after a panic attack, but it worked.

She needed to organize her thoughts. The brick through the window had not seemed like an idle threat. And while she still wanted to help Emily, she needed to be careful.

So, what exactly did she know?

Emily had come to town for a three-month stay. She hadn't brought much furniture. The landlord knew Emily, hadn't seen her in a few days, and hadn't asked Taylor about the mysterious injured girl. That said, the landlord had a son who was single. Evan lived in town but was gone on construction jobs out of town a lot. She was the perfect example of what Sissy had talked about.

Emily had ended up behind Flour Sax while wrapped in a quilt. Perhaps she had wandered there, or maybe she'd been dumped there. No one in the shop had heard anyone drive into the alley. But people did drive electric cars, even in Comfort.

The quilt had come from that farmhouse out by Moon Creek. It had been sold by Klaus, who could give someone a concussion by looking at them cross-eyed. He said he'd sold it to a short, dark woman, but hadn't been clear about what that meant. Hair? Skin? Taylor wasn't sure. Considering Klaus was over six feet tall and blonder than anyone Taylor had ever seen, almost anyone could fit that description. But if she were being honest, Emily was only medium height and fair. No one would have called her short and dark.

And the brick through the window made it clear someone was afraid. Taylor's poking around was getting close.

And finally, she knew the someone in town who was naturally dark, had been asking questions about how long amnesia could last.

Her stack of facts wasn't very tall. If she really was close to finding out what happened, she couldn't see it. She turned her head side to side and then rolled her shoulders hoping to relax her muscles.

What did she really know about this Emily Donner?

She had a brother who was supposed to arrive today. And she had parents who were visiting family in Denmark.

Denmark was Scandinavian. Could there be a connection between Emily and the people who were renovating the farmhouse? Maybe. That was something she could ask Emily's brother.

She also knew that the name Phillip had triggered some kind of memory for Emily. In fact, it had made Emily ask if the Phillip in question was a redhead.

Could that be something? Maybe it was nothing, but it was a thread she hadn't followed up on yet. She wished she hadn't hung up on Sissy so quickly, since Sissy herself claimed she knew everyone in town. She'd know if there was a redhead around here named Phillip. In the meantime, Taylor had both a town directory from about ten years ago, and her own high school yearbook. Between those two resources, she ought to be able to track down a Phillip in this haystack.

# CHAPTER SEVEN

By the time Taylor had scoured every resource in her little house on Love Street, she had a thundering headache.

Now she was slumped over the old pine wood table in the kitchen. She had the town directory spread before her and not just her yearbook, but her mother's yearbooks and her sister's most recent elementary school yearbook.

She'd found a few people named Phil, or Phillip, and one family of Phillips. She'd called the number for the Phillips family, but it wasn't in service.

"Taylor, you were out like a light when I came home." Grandpa Ernie was puttering around the kitchen. "I thought you'd be with your grandmother." He stared at her face as though her injured nose was a bad guy who needed intimidating. "You ought to be somewhere where someone could take care of you."

"I needed some information. I was looking for people called Phillip or Phillips. The name triggered some kind of memory in Emily."

"Only Phil I know, is Phil Dorney." Grandpa Ernie shoved his hands in his pockets and leaned against the wall. She'd noticed him doing that more and more lately.

"Is Phil Dorney related to Sissy?

"Of course. It's her husband."

This shouldn't have been news to Taylor, but she did wonder sometimes if she purposefully blacked out information related to town. Right before her father died, the town had a growth spurt. During the peak of the quilting passion, two new subdivisions had almost doubled the town's size. Sometimes she felt like she knew everything about Comfort, but three thousand people was a big crowd to keep track of. And perhaps that itch to move away kept her from trying to remember everybody. Perhaps.

Then again, maybe she just didn't have the best memory in the whole world.

"Does Sissy know this girl is involved with her husband?"

"That's quite a leap, Grandpa."

"Not if you knew how Sissy and Phil met."

"I'm sure there's a story there, but it's not one for today. Unless, of course, Phil Dorney is a redhead." Taylor rubbed her eyes and immediately regretted it.

Grandpa Ernie barked a deep, throaty laugh. "Phil Dorney hasn't had a full head of hair as long as I've known him. What he used to have most certainly wasn't red."

In good news, the mention of Grandma Quinny's offer of shelter reminded her that Grandma knew everybody and everything. It was time to sit down for a long chat. Between the Scandinavian couple and the mysterious redheaded Phillip, they had a lot to discuss.

Taylor slipped into the comfortable, homey, almost McMansion-like farmhouse on the edge of town. Grandma Quinny was tucked away somewhere in the sprawling home.

Emily was on the phone at the kitchen table. Taylor hovered around, listening in while she fixed herself a little snack.

As soon as Emily hung up, Taylor carried her tray of snacks and two cups of tea to the table. "Was that your brother?"

"Yeah." Emily's whole posture spoke of relief, from her relaxed shoulders to the way she had crossed her feet at the ankle.

"Did he help you remember anything good?" Taylor smeared strawberry jam on a Ritz cracker and topped it with a small slice of cheddar, a little treat her grandmother had taught her to love.

"It did! I don't know why I didn't call him sooner. But between your grandmother and Phil, I'm really beginning to get myself back."

"Phil?" Taylor sipped her tea to try to cover choking on her cracker.

"Yeah, isn't it funny? When that lady in the van said something about Phillip, I immediately thought of a scrappy redhead, and of course, that's my brother. All red hair and freckle faced. It's the Scandinavian in us, I guess."

"It'll be nice when he arrives, won't it?"

Emily's jaw tightened. "I don't know. One of the many things I remember about him is that he's an excellent shot. He said he's coming armed and that no one hurts his little sister."

Taylor's mouth opened, but no words came out. She was used to guns. Guns were just a part of rural small-town life, but she wasn't used to people swinging into town looking for a fight. Not that she could blame this man. After all, if anyone on earth even threatened to hurt her kid sister, she'd turn to violence before you could say Second Amendment rights.

"But he's coming, and he's armed, so the sooner we figure out what happened to me, the better for all of us." Emily sipped her tea. She wrinkled her nose and stirred in a spoonful of sugar.

"You mentioned that Grandma Quinny helped you come up with more memories. Anything you'd like to share?"

"We think I came here to work at the flour mill museum."

"What made you have that idea?"

"We called all the stores in town and no one knew me. So, I didn't come for that kind of part-time job. She asked some leading questions, and I remembered I really like history. The photocopy of my driver's license says I'm twenty-one years old, but I don't know if I'm out of college. We thought I might be here on a work study."

Taylor could almost hear Isaiah warning her that something about this was fishy. But who was she to say how a traumatic brain injury looked? This was her first experience with an amnesiac.

"Did your brother tell you if you were enrolled in school?"

"To be honest, I didn't think to ask. I had to send him a selfie, so he knew it was really me. Then he wanted to tell me our whole life story. Some of it I totally remembered, but I swear he had to be making half of it up. After that, I had to try to talk him down from bringing a posse of his friends and their guns to hunt down the guy who hit me. The whole idea makes me sick."

"'Hit me' is an interesting phrase," Taylor mused. Perhaps Emily's subconscious mind knew she'd been punched.

"You sound like your grandmother," Emily said with a laugh. "I'm so sorry about what happened to your shop, and your face."

Taylor fluttered her fingers near her nose. "I'm sorry about that, too. I think at least the brick should remind us to be careful. I agree your brother bringing a bunch of armed guys is a bad idea. But it might be smart to spread the word that someone is looking out for you. Someone with a little more firepower than a fiber artist and her grandmother."

"This has been a lot of trouble for someone who's moved here to work for a museum." Emily pursed her lips.

"That's all just a guess. It could have been anything." Taylor played with some ideas and then popped out with, "Could you have met someone online?"

Emily's cheeks turned pink.

"Let me guess: Grandma Quinny didn't think to ask that."

Emily pressed her hand to her chest. "My heart is beating a mile a minute. I'd swear it's a panic attack, and I've never had one before. Oh my gosh. I think I came here for a man." She looked disgusted. "What if all this trouble is because I met some man on the internet? How absolutely mortifying."

Taylor laughed. She couldn't help it. She'd been injured in the line of duty. This woman had amnesia. Flour Sax was boarded up, and Emily's biggest worry was being mortified to have met someone online.

How else were you supposed to meet someone?

"There are definitely worse things in the world than this. I promise." Taylor shrugged because it was literally no big deal. "So, you think you might have seen someone online and come to Comfort. I wonder if the apartment was for both of you. Maybe he's not from around here."

"No offense, but I can't imagine sneaking away to a quilt town with a lover. He must be local." Emily scarfed another cracker without cheese or jam. "Maybe I took a job at the museum because I needed income for the summer?"

"Your brother didn't tell you what kind of work you did back home, did he?"

"We only talked about stuff like stupid things our parents used to say, and family vacations, and pets. Phil also had a bunch of memories about shows we used to watch, but I swear he remembers a different TV schedule than I do."

"That sounds like my family reunions." Taylor's mom was an only child, but her father had been one of six kids. When everyone got together, things could get noisy. No one seemed to remember stories the same way, and they loved to argue about who was right.

"So, speaking of meeting someone, what's your type?"

Emily shrugged.

"Don't think too hard. Close your eyes, and picture someone handsome."

Emily did as she was told, then said, "Brad Pitt." Her eyes popped open, and she looked pleased. "Definitely Brad Pitt."

"Not bad! What do you like about Brad Pitt?"

"He's tall and fit. Remember him in *Thelma and Louise?* With that golden-blond hair hanging in his big, blue eyes?"

Taylor was certain few women would forget Brad Pitt in his breakout role. "Try it again."

"Heath Ledger!"

"Another blue-eyed blond. I think we might have discovered your type." Taylor bit the inside of her cheek. One tall blond who had been very reticent about his activities came immediately to mind, and she did not like it.

"Movie stars?" Emily snickered. She was still pink cheeked but looked a little more comfortable. "I would totally be open to dating a brunette, but I did immediately think of more fair-haired men, didn't I?"

"You sure did. I wonder if you found someplace online that specialized in them." Taylor sipped her tea with fake innocence.

Emily rolled her eyes but smiled brightly. "Let's see, there's Match.com, Bumble, Plenty of Fish, but it wasn't any of those." She paused for a long time.

"What about eHarmony?"

"Nah... wait. Hold on. I booked the apartment for all summer, didn't I?"

Taylor nodded.

"Summerfling.com." This time, Emily's face went deep red. "My gosh. It was summerfling.com. I even remember my password. This isn't embarrassing; it's absolutely humiliating. If my parents find out I used the internet to set up a summer fling, they'd disown me."

"They might not have to know." Taylor gave her a hopeful little smile. "But it looks like we are about to get some answers."

# CHAPTER EIGHT

E mily's brother was the kind of handsome that made you think you could fall in love. He was a liberally freckled redhead, though his hair was more auburn, and he had thick, dark brows. But the feature you couldn't turn away from were his big, gray eyes. A sort of steely gray with a black ring around the iris and thick dark lashes. Those big eyes give him a sensitive, vulnerable look. But Taylor doubted he would be vulnerable in a fight. He wasn't much taller than Taylor's five feet eight inches, and he wasn't particularly big, but he moved with an athletic grace, and the cut of his shirt and his jeans left no doubt that he was all muscle. Taylor was staring. But neither Phillip nor Emily seemed to notice.

"I am so glad you came alone. I would've died of embarrassment if you had brought your friends."

"You can't even remember who my friends are." Those big, gray eyes of Phillip's looked sad as he said it, not angry. "But they remember you. Everyone's kid sister, everyone's favorite girl. They're literally a text message away, and they are ready to fight."

Phillip had arrived first thing that morning. He was a day later than he'd said he be, and he had no explanation for his timing or why he was alone. Though he'd practically stormed the Quinn farm like he was rescuing his sister from them, he had been welcomed with open arms by Grandma Quinny.

He'd wasted no time quizzing his sister on the situation, while Grandma Quinny had disappeared to get reinforcements.

"Who did this to you?" He spun and stared at Taylor. "How did you not see? This happened in your own backyard."

Suddenly Phillip wasn't quite as attractive as he had been moments before.

"We don't know anything about where it happened." Taylor shifted from one foot to the other. This was the same thing she'd been beating herself up about for the last few days. How had she not seen or heard Emily arrive in her alley?

"Phillip, it's not her fault. For all we know, I wandered quietly and collapsed. In fact, it would have to be that, because nobody heard a car, and if nobody heard anything, then it didn't happen. This is just normal deduction, isn't it?"

"The important thing isn't what we've missed," Taylor said, "but what we've learned. So far we know where she got the quilt, and we know why she came to Comfort."

Emily shot daggers at Taylor. They had not logged into the dating site last night. Taylor and Emily had both just hurt too badly. They couldn't bring themselves to do it. They knew they had the morning. What could one night change? With Phillip's early morning arrival, it turned out one night could change a lot.

"The museum. A job," Emily blurted out.

"That's stupid." Phillip curled his lip in disgust. "You haven't worked anywhere but the family business since you quit Target. Why would you work for a museum? Were you even getting paid? Do museums ever pay people?"

His allure was definitely fading. Not that Taylor was a mad fan of history, but his absolute disdain for it turned her stomach.

Emily caught Taylor's eye, and Taylor saw the similarity between the siblings. Emily's eyes were round and vulnerable and scared. Taylor shrugged. They had to log in to the dating site. They had to find out who she'd come here to meet. And since Phillip was here, there was no hiding it from him. But at the same time, it wasn't Taylor's decision to make.

Grandma Quinny came back to the kitchen with Grandpa Quinny in tow. "We're so glad you've come. I hope you will consider staying with us."

Grandpa Quinny glanced quickly at Taylor as though looking for confirmation of some kind.

She lifted one shoulder in a half-hearted shrug. What kind of confirmation did Grandpa want? That Phillip was safe to have in the house? How on earth would Taylor know?

"You must be the brother," Grandpa Quinny said sternly.

"Yes, sir. Phillip Donner. I'm Emily's older brother. It doesn't sound like the cops are doing anything about the man who hurt my sister."

Grandpa Quinny didn't let down his guard. "What do you intend to do about that, young man?"

"Find him. Turn him over to the police. Apparently, my sister doesn't appreciate my ability to take care of him myself." His mouth quirked into a rueful smile.

Grandpa Quinny's stern look turned into a glower. "I agree with your sister. I hope you didn't come here intending to do violence."

"How would you feel if this was your sister?" Phillip challenged him.

Taylor cringed. Nobody challenged Grandpa Quinny. Grandpa Quinny grew strawberries. Grandpa Quinny invited the kindergarten class to his farm every year for an outing. Grandpa Quinny bent over backward to please his wife. And Grandpa Quinny didn't put up with nonsense. Who did this Phillip think he was?

"If I were your age, perhaps, I would also find it difficult to restrain myself." Grandpa Quinny gave Taylor a long paternal look.

"But with time comes wisdom. Now I know violence would make things worse."

Phillip flexed his jaw, but his eyes softened again. "I said what I said. I'm here to find out who did this and turn them into the police. I didn't pack a gun."

"But you've got a baseball bat in your car."

Phillip smiled. "And the glove and the ball, sir."

Grandpa Quinny scoffed.

Phillip grimaced.

Emily was definitely not going to mention the dating site in front of Taylor's grandparents.

Taylor cleared her throat. "I'd like to take them to Reuben's, if you don't mind. We'll get a private booth and have a chat."

Grandma Quinny frowned. "We can chat privately far more easily here."

"Sure." Taylor grasped for a way to make this less insulting to her grandmother. "But if we drive through town, she might remember something new. That's all."

"Let the kids go, Ingrid." Grandpa Quinny put his arm around his wife.

She didn't argue, but she stood on the front porch and watched them drive away.

Emily and Taylor took a booth at the back of the diner. Phillip walked up and down the block and then around the building, casing the joint. Taylor leaned across the table and kept her voice low. "We need to tell him about the dating site."

Emily nodded and opened her menu, but she didn't look at it. "I know, but I think he's going to hate it."

"Do you remember him well now? Is he always like this? He seems really agitated."

"Yeah, I basically remember all of my early life now. The doctor said it would come back fast, and he was right. As far as I remember, Phil's always been like this. A bit of a hair trigger, a tantrum thrower. I think when we were kids, they called it oppositional defiance disorder. I don't know. He takes medicine."

"Was he violent with you ever?"

"No more than a normal brother. He never hit me or strangled me or anything like that. We wrestled a little, and raced, and oh, I'm sure he tripped me when he shouldn't have. He saved his outbursts for people in authority. In other words, I'm one hundred percent certain he's not the one who assaulted me."

Phillip strode back in like he was in charge, so they quickly picked up their menus.

"I guess I'll just have the three-pancake meal." Emily smiled at her brother.

"And I'll have the truth." Phillip crossed his arms and stared down at his sister. "What is going on here?"

Emily and Taylor locked eyes. Taylor lifted her eyebrows, pinched her lips a little, and nodded, hoping to give Emily some encouragement. She hadn't practiced the art of persuasive facial expressions before, but it seemed to work.

Emily took a deep breath, straightened her shoulders, looked at her hands, and then spoke very quietly. "I met someone on a site called summerfling.com. I'm so embarrassed, Phil. But I just wanted to have a little fun. I was tired of going out and getting ghosted. It always seems like men just want one-night stands."

"A summer fling isn't any better." Phil's nostrils flared.

"You might think that, but it's humiliating to never get past that first date. I hate thinking we had a good time but never hearing from them again. I thought at least with a summer fling, I could have three whole months of romance. And maybe I'm naïve, but it seemed like if I spent the summer with someone, it could turn into more. Maybe I don't make a great first impression, but if someone took the time to actually get to know me, it could've worked out."

The outpouring of emotion surprised Taylor. For someone with so little memory, she sure got to the heart of her hopes and dreams quickly. The revelation startled Taylor, but the logic tracked. And secretly, Taylor had been hoping for the same thing in grad school. She thought it would be lovely to meet someone right away and have a couple of years to fall in love.

On the other hand, this was a remarkable bit of amnesia recovery. In fact, it seemed more than likely Emily had been faking, if not all of her memory loss, then at least most of it. She had so quickly remembered her parents, who would have been easy for the police to find. And not very long after that, she claimed to remember her entire childhood. All the easy-to-check stuff, Emily had managed to fit into her narrative pretty quickly.

The only things she couldn't remember were the parts that embarrassed her.

Taylor could also appreciate this. She had plenty of things in life she wished the rest of the world could forget. She wondered if Emily knew exactly who had assaulted her. Perhaps she was scared to tell the truth.

"You'd better log in and figure out who you matched with." Phillip passed Emily his phone.

Emily did the deed in silence, seeming to remember her log-in and password with ease. Eventually, she found a picture of a strikingly handsome, icy-blond Scandinavian type.

Taylor was not one bit surprised to see Klaus's smug face on that screen. "Did you know he was married?" she asked quietly.

"He's married?"

Phil slammed both fists on the table. "Enough games, Emily. This man hurt you, and he's gonna pay for it."

"It wasn't him. I'm sure of it. We never even met."

"But the amnesia." Taylor lifted one eyebrow.

"It maybe wasn't as bad as I claimed it was. But it did take me a few days to remember why I was here. I didn't make that up. I cannot remember what happened or how I ended up behind your store. I remember driving to town. I remember renting the apartment. I don't remember getting a job at the museum, so that's just a bit of conjecture. I suppose we can check it out."

"I don't see why you would've needed a job," Phil interjected. "You've got tons of money."

"I don't feel inside like the kind of person who wouldn't work for the whole summer. But I guess if I can't remember what job I was planning on doing, there's a good chance there wasn't one." Emily scrunched her mouth. She looked annoyed, as though she honestly didn't remember her job in the family business.

"Before today, I didn't think you were the kind of girl who'd run away with a stranger from the internet." Phil curled his lip in disgust, but there was a tiny sparkle of humor in his eyes.

"If it means anything, I swear I did not know he was married. But I do know that we hadn't met. Pretty quickly after we talked to the landlord, it all came back to me. Or as much of it as was possible, I guess. I remembered getting the apartment. I remembered looking around for apartment stuff. I remember thinking the antique mall was too expensive to buy furniture for a short stay. Maybe if I'd wanted to keep them, or if they were fine antiques or something, but that wasn't what I was after. I do remember that much, and I remember lengthy phone calls at night. He has an amazing voice. We made plans to meet in town."

"Idiot," Phil muttered.

Taylor agreed. What kind of man met his secret lover in a small town where he lived?

"The details are fuzzy. We were going to meet for coffee. Probably at that little place up the street... what's it called? Cup of Joe's, I think? He said he was embarrassed to have met someone online and wanted us to pretend like we were old friends."

"That's a bit suspicious. Sounds like a man who wanted to establish a reason to talk to you so that people in town wouldn't think he was cheating on his wife." Phil rapped his knuckles on the table. He looked as though he was dying to hit something.

"It sounded weird to me, too, but I mean, nothing about this was normal, was it?"

Phil threw his hands in the air. "This is ridiculous, absurd, and dangerous. I'm going to meet this guy and tell him what I think."

"I guess so. I mean, if he really did assault me... oh, I don't know. I don't remember meeting him at the coffee shop. I remember making the plans. I remember driving over to this area, and then I remember waking up in pain in an ambulance. Everything else is just not there. I swear I'm not trying to protect this guy. I promise."

Phil snorted. He made as though to stand. He looked around the room with fire in those clear gray eyes.

"Are you planning to attack him because you think he did this? Or is it because he's married?"

"Both are good enough for me." Phil might be filled with righteous anger, but he was a lot smaller than Klaus. He looked like he'd lose that fight.

"I guess I report this all to the police, huh?"

"That's entirely up to you, Emily. But think of this: You were assaulted, and my shop was vandalized. I highly doubt Klaus would do all of that if what he wanted was a summer fling."

The look of frustrated anger that Phil gave Taylor implied that he agreed with Taylor, and he hated it.

# CHAPTER NINE

After their breakfast, Taylor went straight to Flour Sax and spent the whole day there.

Emily had Phil to look after her. Phil had Grandma and Grandpa Quinny to keep an eye on him.

Emily had decisions to make.

Taylor considered calling the police herself to share the information about Klaus, since Flour Sax was a victim of this little crime spree. But honestly, no matter how badly she wanted someone to blame, she just didn't think it was him.

"Good night, Taylor. I'm heading out. You coming home tonight, or are you going to the Quinn's farm again?" Grandpa Ernie asked with one hand on the doorknob.

"I'll come home, I think. Grandma and Grandpa Quinny have their hands full. I thought I'd go over the books one more time before I left." She laughed. "I need the practice. They didn't offer many business classes at the craft college, but I did take all of them."

"You do live the wild life." Grandpa Ernie laughed. "I talked to your mom today. She's about ready to get on an airplane and come home. You should call her. She can't believe you haven't called her back."

"I texted." Taylor blushed. She ought to have called her mom back, and she knew it.

"She tried to call again today."

"I still have my phone on silent—a habit from school. If she leaves Belle for this nonsense, I'll just be sick. I'll check my messages and call her. See you back home."

Once Ernie was long gone, and Taylor had gone over the month's books, she was out of excuses to ignore her phone.

There was, of course, a long voicemail from her mom. Laura Quinn, Taylor's young, beautiful mother was not much for texting. And so, more often than not, Taylor did miss her calls. "Taylor, darling, you have to call me. I didn't like that the shop was damaged, because it made me worried for you. They could burn it to the ground, but so long as you were safe, I'd be okay. Now Grandpa says you've been injured. If you don't call me back, I will immediately fly home. You know I will because you know I love you with my whole heart. I couldn't love anything or anyone more than you and our Belly-Bean, and I have been here with her having a great time, so she knows that I love her. But you—oh, never mind. I'm rambling. I promise if you don't call me back tonight, I will be on the first flight, no matter the cost. Love you, darling."

Taylor groaned. She adored her mother. Laura Quinn was a great gal, good friend, hard worker, and all the rest of the superlatives belonged to her mother, too. But the last thing Taylor wanted was her mother to take over.

And yet she didn't call. Those kinds of calls could last forever, and Taylor wasn't sure she had the energy for it. That was her excuse anyway. Instead, she sent a quick text: *Mom, I'm okay. I didn't even get stitches. I love you with my whole heart, too. Take lots of pictures. Please don't abandon Belle for this.* She was about to delete her mom's voicemail when she reconsidered. It was a nice message. It wouldn't hurt to keep it for a little while.

She felt a little guilty for texting again instead of calling, so she made a quick call to Grandma Quinny.

After greeting Taylor, Grandma Quinny launched straight into the news of the day. "Those two have been fighting nonstop. It's like having my own kids back. You and the girl never fought, but that's probably because of the age difference."

Taylor snorted. Grandma Quinny still referred to Belle as "the girl" sometimes. It was weird, but she swore she only did it because there were so many Isabellas/Bellas/Belles in the family after that Disney movie had come out. Since Grandma Quinny's family extended to include cousins of cousins, new partners of divorced cousins, and cousins of new partners of divorced cousins, a family tree for Grandma Quinny could include the whole world. In that case, it was true there were too many Belles to keep track of.

"Tell me you listened in. We need to know everything they've been fighting about." Taylor settled in, ready for a story.

"Phillip runs with a dangerous crowd, and he really wants to bring them all here to Comfort."

"If they all look like Phil, the ladies of Comfort won't be sorry about this."

Grandma Quinny laughed again. "He is a handsome fellow. Do you want me to find out if he's single?"

"No way. He's way too angry for me. I could never have a relationship with someone like that."

"All you kids jump to relationships so quickly. I was merely thinking you might like someone to take down to Loggers for a drink and some dancing. Summer will be long if you don't socialize."

Grandma Quinny was the last person Taylor would have suspected of endorsing a summer fling. It was surprising and kind of sweet.

"If his mob of angry friends show up, I can always take one of them out for a drink and some dancing."

"You could do worse," Grandma Quinny stated.

Taylor paused. Maybe Phil's friends weren't violent and scary. Maybe one of them was cute and nice. Not that there weren't cute boys in town already. Hudson East, all grown up and running around fixing things, popped into her mind. But that was different somehow. You didn't have a fling with someone from your hometown. You had a relationship, and you stuck with it, or an awful lot of people could get hurt.

"Besides his friends, did they fight about anything else? Any other news?"

"She can't decide if she wants to press charges or not. Very foolish, if you ask me. She needs to contact this man and find out if he met her at the coffee shop, and go from there."

"She can't press charges till she knows what happened, can she?"

"That is still the weak point. Clever you for spotting it." Grandma Quinny was teasing. It was a comfortable but also nettling sort of thing. Familiar, if nothing else.

She might as well have called her mother, but Laura wouldn't have teased and nettled her. She would have gushed and babied her, and that was irritating in a whole different way.

"Maybe instead of Emily pressing charges, you and I should," Taylor suggested softly.

The thought was met with a moment of silence, followed immediately with firm agreement. "Taylor Quinn, you are a delight. You and I will call on them first thing tomorrow morning."

"Grandma, he might be at work. We don't know his schedule."

"Your morning and my morning must be very different. There's no way this man will have left by the time I plan on being there."

GRANDMA QUINNY HAD NOT BEEN MESSING AROUND. She and Taylor stood on the front porch of the farmhouse out by Moon Creek slightly before six the next morning. After a few knocks, Lonnie came to the door. Dark shadows hung under her eyes, but she was already dressed. "What?"

"Is your husband at home?" Grandma Quinny asked.

"Yes." Lonnie offered them the sort of one-word welcome Taylor thought they deserved for arriving that early.

"You might want to bring him downstairs for little chat with us." Grandma Quinny's tone indicated this wasn't a request.

Lonnie turned to Taylor. "That was an accident. You said you weren't going to lay charges against him."

"I'm certainly not going to lay those charges against him. It does hurt though." Taylor fluttered her fingers in front of her damaged nose. "And I think a conversation might make it feel a lot better."

"Come, sit in the kitchen. I just made a pot of coffee. I'll get Klaus." Her shoulders sank a little, and she trudged through the house.

"We've made it this far," Taylor said as soon as Lonnie left. "What's next?"

"Leave it to me, my dear. We're going to have a conversation and lead it to where we need it to go."

This seemed a bold statement, considering how things had gone last time.

Lonnie and Klaus returned together, both dressed, and both looking stormy.

"This conversation isn't going to be pleasant for you," Grandma Quinny said, addressing Lonnie. "But it's probably something you should know about."

"If it's about our construction mess, you have to take it up with him." Lonnie tilted her head in Klaus's direction.

"Pardon? "Grandma Quinny lifted an eyebrow.

"We've had people here on and off all week asking about the pile of bricks in the back."

"And the pile of wood," Klaus agreed.

"Everyone wants a piece of this house, and everyone has such a good reason that they deserve it for free. I'm sick to death of it. I know it's a mess; half the neighbors come here to ask us when we'll finally haul it away, but for heaven's sake, every other farm on this road looks like a trash pile. Why can't we for a little while?" Lonnie took a long drink of her coffee.

"Who was asking about the bricks?" Taylor asked.

"Hipster trash. They want the old bricks from the garage we tore down. They assume they've discovered some hundred-year-old treasure when really the garage was put up in the seventies. The bricks were just a façade."

"Not full-sized bricks, then?" Taylor tried to play it cool, but she was disappointed. The brick that had taken out her window had definitely been big.

"They were full-size bricks, but the garage was stick built. Some idiot who didn't know what he was doing put a brick façade on the front. He made a real hash of it, and the wood structure behind it was rotten. We had to tear it down. That's what the mess is."

"Did you end up giving any of the bricks away?" Taylor was on the edge of her seat, rubbing her index finger back and forth across the ribbed linen table runner. Nervous energy spilled out of her.

"No way. Everyone wanted free bricks. Someone even suggested I pay them to haul the bricks away. They probably wanted to resell them—like my quilt, apparently."

"Dear God, if I hear about that quilt one more time! I promise you I will buy it back." Klaus's voice was rich with indignation. "Didn't you people say you knew who had it?"

If he was pretending not to know who had the quilt, he was doing a ridiculously good job.

Lonnie waved away Klaus's contribution to the conversation. "Well, anyway, a handful of people came asking about the bricks. One girl seemed more... I don't know... she just seemed more realistic about things. She said she wanted a sample to take home to her husband, so I gave her one. No one else wanted a sample."

"When did this happen?" Excitement tickled at Taylor's heart. A woman who wanted just one brick? This seemed like a great place to dig a little deeper.

"When was the rainstorm, Klaus? She came that day. I remember she was soaking wet, and I wanted to get her out of the rain."

"I don't know. A few days ago."

Taylor, on the other hand, remembered exactly the day of the rainstorm. That had been the day before she got a brick through the window of her shop.

"What did she look like?" Taylor's voice was tight as she tried to contain herself.

Grandma Quinny gently tapped her foot on top of Taylor's, but Taylor lifted her eyebrows and pressed her lips together. They were onto something here.

"She wore a striped knit cap. Almost all of her hair was tucked up in it, but some dark strands were poking out the back. The stripes were sort of ombre, red, orange, and yellow. Very trendy looking. Let's see, she had hazel eyes and an olive complexion. The brick was really big in her hands, so I'd say she was petite. She wore a stack of silver rings on one finger."

Klaus put his hands on Lonnie's shoulder and looked proud. "Lonnie has an incredible eye for detail." But after saying that, he swallowed nervously.

Why did Taylor think he looked nervous? Just because she saw his Adam's apple bob up and down? She wasn't used to seeing Adam's apples. Anyone was allowed to swallow. That didn't mean he was nervous. But it stuck with her anyway. Lonnie's great memory made him nervous.

Lonnie shifted from his touch. "I remember most everything I see. She also had long fingernails but not polished, just nicely filed. She wore a pair of low-top Converse in"—she tilted her head—"pink, I think, possibly salmon."

"Now she's showing off," Klaus said with a laugh. "We're going to be here a while if she tells you everything. Let me get you some coffee." He must've meant it, because he gave everyone a hot mug and settled into a chair at the table. He had apparently sat in on his wife's lengthy descriptions before.

By the time they were ready to leave, they had every detail down to the little mole by the woman's left ear. But even better, they had her license plate number. At the door, as the couple were trying to usher them out, Grandma Quinny had one more thing to say: "We know about summerfling.com."

The man swallowed again. His Adam's apple bobbed up and down in exactly the same way it had before, but this time Taylor felt positive it was nerves.

"Well..." Lonnie sighed. "It goes to figure. We are legally separated."

"Lonnie…" Klaus's voice was rough.

"I should probably get around to filing for divorce. Klaus is just not a one-woman man, and that's not for me."

"The girl who was assaulted outside my shop and found wrapped in the quilt you made in middle school, matched with him on summerfling.com. She said she was supposed to meet him at a coffee shop but doesn't remember doing it."

Lonnie slumped against the wall. "Who's going to come stay at my little bed-and-breakfast now, Klaus? Everyone is going to think that I attacked this kid in a jealous rage." She caught Taylor's eye. "I'm not a violent woman. My petty revenge was using the last of our savings to buy this farm and making him remodel it for me."

"I would've done that anyway," Klaus said. "I adore you, and if we weren't married, you would absolutely be one of my favorite girlfriends." He reached out to pat her shoulder with a devilish twinkle in his eye.

Lonnie jerked away. "One of the best parts about this house is that nasty basement where I make him sleep. But this is it. This is the last straw. You're staying here for at least six months so the whole community knows what an amicable divorce we are having.

I would never hurt anyone, and you're going to make sure the world knows it."

"She really wouldn't," Klaus agreed. He turned to Grandma Quinny and Taylor. Though he looked a little nervous, he looked more embarrassed. It was the weirdest thing, like maybe he was a afraid of losing the sweet deal he had managed: beautiful wife and ladies on the side. "She's a nurse. An excellent nurse. She generally works with the elderly and was just hired to work at Bible Creek Care Home. This bed-and-breakfast is her dream, and I bet she makes it come true."

"Anything else in our family life you'd like to share with these absolute strangers, Klaus?" Lonnie nudged him with her elbow in an almost playful move.

"Seems to me they know everything anyway." Klaus took a few steps forward using his physical presence to push them out the door. Taylor didn't mind. She'd had as much of their troubles as she could handle.

Once she was buckled up in her grandmother's car, she asked the big question: "I suppose we go to the police with the description and license plate number to find the girl who put the brick through my window?"

"I doubt one girl taking one brick will be seen as convincing evidence. But we don't need their help to identify her anyway. That's just Lindsay Donahue. She works at Cuppa Joe's. She's the one with those silly blue streaks in her hair."

"Blue streaks? Like the girl I saw in Target." Emily's face flushed. "No wonder I couldn't take my eyes off her."

Though the hour was still absurdly early, Taylor and Grandma Quinny found Emily awake and having breakfast when they returned home. They wasted no time informing her of all they'd learned.

"That young lady Lonnie really does have a good eye for detail. By the time she'd described Lindsay's knit cap, I knew exactly who she was talking about."

Taylor didn't know Lindsay, not really. She wasn't able to guess what had happened based on a knowledge of the barista's personality. Yet she could see the whole thing now. She could see it like a quilt top whose squares had finally been put together to reveal a second pattern. Lindsay Donahue was a barista. People made all sorts of phone calls in the coffee shop. She could have heard Emily making a date with Klaus. And with a name like Klaus, if Lindsay had also matched with him, she'd have recognized it and been jealous. And her romantic envy had caused her to go a little haywire.

But how was Taylor going to convince the police?

She had hoped for some sort of dramatic moment where Emily remembered everything, but it hadn't happened.

Emily sat at the kitchen table, wrapped up in the secondhand quilt. Her bowl of cereal was mostly untouched. Her brother, Phil, joined them after a moment.

"Honest to gosh, though, I still can't believe this quilt wasn't actually mine. I just have a really strong sense of nostalgia attached to it." She held the edge of it to her cheek.

"You're an idiot." Phil picked up the blanket edge and flipped it back and forth. "Those geese were the curtains in Grandma's kitchen. She had, like, a goose shrine."

"How on earth do you remember grandma's kitchen curtains?" Emily traced the outline of one of the white geese.

"To start with, I was at her house last weekend. She's gotten rid of the curtains, but she still has all the canisters and the framed picture on the wall. How do you not remember the geese in your own grandmother's kitchen?"

"Amnesia?" she said with a smile.

"Mom and Dad should never have gotten you that phone in elementary school. I swear you never look up and see what's around you."

"I never did love the geese look," Grandma Quinny said. "It's strawberries all the way for me."

"I've noticed. But I bet she hasn't." Phil kicked his sister's foot. "I think you were at Cuppa Joe's having coffee and talking to Klaus. The barista heard you and got jealous."

"Okay, sure. I don't remember the barista, but I did have coffee there. According to the lease papers, I'd been in town two days before the assault. Realistically, I could have been having coffee at the café and talking to Klaus on the phone at the same time. But how did the barista lure me to a dark corner? I was assaulted in the middle of the day."

"You were shopping for housewares and stuff, weren't you?" Taylor asked.

"I was looking for some stuff."

"Check your phone log," Phil demanded.

Emily held out her very rudimentary burner phone. "If I had *my* phone, we'd have gotten to the bottom of this a long time ago. As much as I appreciate this one, it doesn't have any contacts, texts, or a call log from before the assault."

Grandma Quinny got up suddenly, and grabbed a thin local newspaper from the top of the burn pile. "This will have the answers, I'm sure. Check the classifieds. Look for furniture that sounds like it's your taste."

"But how would the barista have slipped an ad in the classifieds in time to assault her?" Taylor asked. "Don't these come out once a week?"

"They come out twice a month," Grandma Quinny corrected. "The barista didn't have to place an ad. All she had to do was listen while Emily called and made an appointment. Simple as anything."

"I bet we find Emily's car stripped of its plates not far from the furniture she wanted to buy," Taylor said.

"Nope," Phil said. "The car is long gone. Even if the person who'd assaulted her had no use for it, someone else's stolen it by now."

Emily shook the paper to get their attention. "I would've liked this one. Danish modern coffee table and dining chair. I bet I could have fit those in the back of my car, too. I'd have wanted that even in Portland. And for this price, I'd have bought it to resell, if nothing else. We should call just to find out if they still have it." Emily had a hungry look in her eye as she smiled down at the paper. "I'll call right now."

To Emily's disappointment, the furniture had sold, but the seller did give the address—a house on Love Street, less than a block from the corner where Flour Sax was located.

"The McGoverns," Grandma Quinny murmured. "They have that awful row of arborvitae in front of their house. Anything could happen in that driveway, and no one would be the wiser."

"I don't know if anything happened or not. I really don't remember." Emily's face scrunched in annoyance. She gripped the quilt in her two fists. "But if I thought I was getting the chair and table, I'd have backed my car up as close to the door as I could to make it easier to load."

"Yup," Phil agreed. "I've seen you on the hunt. You get straight down to business."

They sat in silence for just a moment, and then, with wise interjections from Grandma Quinny, they made a plan.

# CHAPTER TEN

Taylor sent a text to Phillip: *Okay, I think I'm ready.* She wasn't sure if she was thrilled or terrified by the risk they were about to take. Either way, the plan had been set in motion, and she wasn't going to turn back. Emily was safely hidden in the apartment above Flour Sax. Phillip was on his way to Cuppa Joe's. And Taylor was stationed at the back door of her store. As soon as she was given the signal, she would ring Phillip, and he would work his hardest to set a little fire under Lindsay Donahue.

Taylor paced in a small circle with her grandfather's recliner at the center of it. The wait for her cue to call felt like hours, and yet when she got the thumbs-up, it was suddenly too soon. Anything could go wrong now, and anyone could get hurt. But she buttoned up her fear just long enough to make the call.

"Phillip, it's Taylor." She spoke as loud as she could and hoped her voice would carry.

"Taylor, I'm glad you called." Part of the plan was to say each other's names more often than was natural, so Lindsay would know exactly who was talking. He also spoke louder than a normal person, but since no one knew him, she hoped it would come across as just more of that aggressive macho thing he had going.

"Emily Donner remembers." Taylor leaned heavily on the recliner. Her grandfather was safe at the little house down the street, and she had a plan to defend herself. She just needed to keep that in mind. This was a good, safe plan.

"You say my sister, Emily, remembered something? What?"

"*Everything*," Taylor said. "She remembers *everything*."

"You'd better call the police," Phil practically shouted the demand.

"No, no, not yet," Taylor said. "She's scared. She won't even tell me what she remembers."

"Then I'm gonna come right down there and make her tell us. We can finally put her fears to rest."

"She's stubborn, Phillip. You know that. She's your sister."

"Is she at Flour Sax with you now?" Phil asked, ratcheting his volume back up.

"She is. I've gotta leave her here alone though. Grandpa Ernie needs me back at his house. But I'll lock things up. I think she'll be fine. It's not like anyone can get in."

"You're going to leave her alone at Flour Sax? Are you crazy?" Phil countered in exactly the tone of voice that made Taylor think he would be the worst boyfriend ever. "Anyone could break into your shop. Don't you keep the key under the mat?"

"You'd better not be in public. I don't need half the town knowing where I keep the spare key."

"It's just me and the barista, Taylor." He paused. "And some beefy guy on his cell phone. What's he going to do, steal all your thread?"

A beefy guy on his phone? Phil wasn't supposed to give the signal till he was alone with Lindsay.

"I'm gonna leave in fifteen minutes. Finish your coffee and meet me at my house. Emily will be safe all locked up in the shop." Taylor did her best to sound natural, but she had never been a theater kid, and this acting was not for her.

"Hey, Taylor. You're the absolute best. Did you know that? I promise I won't tell anyone else about the key under the back-door mat. I trust you when you say Emily is safe there all alone. I'll meet you at your house. Hope Grandpa Ernie is okay."

"Thanks, Phillip. See you later." She ended the call and sent him a text: *What do you think? Did she seem to buy it?*

He responded immediately: *She just hung up her apron. She's telling someone in the back that she's taking her lunch.*

Taylor's finger shook as she tapped out her message: *Excellent. You'd better head straight to my house. Make sure she sees you going right past the shop.*

Phillip didn't keep her waiting for a response: *Yeah, I'll make it look good. Don't worry. But I'm not going to leave you with this lunatic for long.*

Taylor took a deep breath and typed slowly: *Emily and I will be fine. Two against one. If Lindsay doesn't have a brick, she can't do much harm. Besides, do you know how many really sharp scissors we have in this place?*

He sent a thumbs-up.

"You good up there?" Taylor hollered to Emily.

Emily sent a thumbs-up via text.

Taylor wanted to chat with her to calm her own nerves, but after a few attempts via text, she gave up. Emily apparently didn't like to chat when she was scared.

Taylor had turned out the lights, and the weak cloud-covered sun coming through the back-door window cast the room in dim, gray shadows.

One of the building's aging pipes let out a low groan.

Taylor's phone made a slight buzz, but it was just an update from an app.

Eventually, the back doorknob rattled.

A flash of heat followed by icy dread flooded Taylor. She ducked around the corner hiding behind the wall of the classroom space.

"Emily?" a small voice called out. "Emily, it's me, Lonnie. We should talk." The voice didn't sound like Lonnie.

"Emily?" the voice called out a little louder. Taylor was almost certain this was Lindsay. She let out a breath.

Now, if only they could get the timing right. Lindsay needed to confess everything, but not until Phil showed up to be another witness.

"Who's there?" Emily called from the top of the stairs. She, it seemed, had been a theater kid. She hit just the right tone of fear and hope.

"Emily, it's me, Lonnie Larsen. Klaus's wife. Come down. We should talk about the girl from the coffee shop. She hurt us both, don't you think?"

The sound of Emily's footsteps on the stairs was Taylor's cue to jump in.

"You're not Lonnie!" Taylor cried as she stepped out from behind the wall.

Lindsay screamed.

"Shh," Emily soothed. "She didn't mean to scare you. Right, Taylor?"

"Sorry." Taylor grinned. Lindsay Donahue was exactly as Lonnie had described her. Petite and nonthreatening. There wasn't a chance she could hurt them. The only risk now was that she wouldn't confess.

"I feel bad for Lonnie." Emily held out her hand as though she wanted to comfort Lindsay.

"You shouldn't," Lindsay snapped and stepped back, bumping into the mini fridge that held up Grandpa Ernie's small black-and-white TV.

"Her husband is a cheater. He found me online. How did he meet you?" Emily asked.

Taylor circled around so she stood between Lindsay and the back door. Any minute Phil should come storming in, ready to be the third witness. As it was, Taylor was poised to dial the police as soon as she needed to.

"They're separated. He didn't do anything wrong." Lindsay spit the words out. "If you'd have just gone back home, you'd have never gotten hurt."

Emily's eyes went wide, and her hand gripped the stair rail. "Oh my gosh. I remember. I remember what happened."

Taylor squeezed her phone. Where was Phil? She should call him to get him here, but then if she needed to call the police... Though she'd told Phil they had plenty of scissors in the shop, she would never have the nerve to stab someone. Instead, she slid her phone into her back pocket and grabbed a bolt of fabric. It was big and heavy. Perfect for a shield or to knock someone on the head.

"You would have done the same thing." Lindsay choked on a sob. "I would do anything for Klaus. It was love at first sight, for me anyway. He's meant to be mine. I just need time. He'll recognize it's true love if he's not distracted with other girls."

Taylor swallowed. His rudimentary description of Lindsay as some short, dark-haired woman who'd bought the quilt hadn't sounded close to true love.

"Taylor, it's all true, isn't it? She heard me set a date with him. And then she heard me make plans to go get that furniture. She... she thought she could talk me out of dating Klaus, or maybe intimidate me. That's what it was, wasn't it? You thought you could talk me out of it."

"You barely gave me a chance to say anything."

Emily was interrupted when the door flung open, and Phil lunged forward, with another big, beefy guy on his tail.

Taylor squinted at the familiar figure as he pushed Phil out of the way. "Taylor?"

"Hudson? What are you doing here?"

"I didn't like the sound of that phone call in the café."

"I tried to talk him out of coming with." Phil was at his sister's side, somewhat in front of her, with what looked to Taylor to be a protective fighting stance.

"Hudson, you really didn't need to come…" Taylor took a breath and counted to five.

Lindsay cut around Grandpa Ernie's chair, moving toward the front of the shop. "You can't keep me here. That's false arrest."

"That's a weird leap to take." Hudson's voice was low and slow.

"She assaulted me." Emily's voice was breathy and fragile sounding. "She pulled me from my car and threatened me. When I wouldn't back down…"

"I didn't threaten you. I just told you how it was. Klaus is meant to be with me, and you needed to go back to where you came from."

"But then you threw me to the ground."

"How was I supposed to know you were so weak?"

Taylor grabbed for her phone, but Phil already had his to his ear.

"What did you tell her, Lindsay? What exactly happened? How did she do this to you?" Taylor kept her voice smooth like she was asking a customer how many yards of fabric she needed.

Hudson was next to her now, and he spoke quietly in her ear, "Taylor, I don't think this is—"

Taylor batted Hudson with her bolt of fabric.

"Ouch."

She held her finger to her lips.

"You could have done that the first time." Hudson backed toward the door, out of her reach.

"I offered to talk," Lindsay said. "I told her I understood why she'd want to see Klaus, but that he was mine, and she needed to go back home. I helped her out of her car."

"She grabbed me by my shirt and dragged me out," Emily corrected.

"I helped her out, and she refused to agree. She refused to talk. She said he could make up his own mind, but that was ridiculous. She was in my space, so I put some distance between us."

"You were holding me by my shirt! I wasn't in your space." Emily's strength seemed to be returning as she countered Lindsay's version of things. "And you didn't put distance between us; you spun me around and threw me down. I think I hit my head on the curb."

"You didn't look hurt to me. You stood up. You seemed a little dizzy, which is your own damn fault, so, I wrapped you in that old blanket I'd bought, pushed you in the direction of the street, and moved your car."

Taylor muttered "quilt" under her breath before she could stop herself.

Lindsay and Emily both turned to her and stared.

"Where did you move her car?" Taylor set the bolt of fabric down and leaned on it. If anything, having two wound-up men made things feel less safe, so she wanted it at hand.

"I parked it by the college. It shouldn't have been hard to find. If she wasn't so weak, she would have followed me down there."

"You gave me a concussion and I passed out! I'm not weak; you're a maniac!"

Lindsay lunged at Emily, but Phil jumped in between them and grabbed her by both shoulders. "You assaulted my sister—you're going to prison for this. Add property damage and stealing her car, and you're in real trouble." He shook Lindsay by the shoulders.

"Hold on," Hudson interjected with a calm voice and a hand to Phil's shoulder.

Phil jerked away from his touch and yanked Lindsay to him, holding her against his chest with one arm, like a kidnapper in a movie. "The police are on their way, and she's going nowhere."

"Of course she's not." Taylor casually picked up the bolt of fabric. "There are four of us here. We all heard the story. We'll press charges. There's no reason to make things worse."

"I didn't steal her car. I just parked it around the corner. She should have followed me, and none of this would have happened. I wouldn't have had to put a brick through your window if you'd just minded your own business." Lindsay twisted in Phil's arms. The narcissistic bend to Lindsay's history of events was impressive. Even throwing a brick through a window hadn't been her own fault.

"There's no reason to hurt her, man." Hudson was moving toward Phil.

Phil grabbed Lindsay by the hair and twisted her so she bent over his arm.

"Ouch! You're hurting me!" Lindsay's face crumpled. She dipped her head and bit his arm, holding on with a vicious grip.

Phil arched his back, lifting Lindsay off her feet. "I'll show you hurt!"

Taylor took a breath, lifted the fabric bolt, and swung it at the side of Phil's head.

He tottered and threw his hands up to protect himself.

Lindsay dropped to the floor and crawled to Hudson. When he helped her up, she threw her arms around him.

He weaseled his way out of her embrace. "It's Taylor you want. She's the one that coldcocked the lunatic."

"Hey!" Emily hollered. "Phil was just protecting me!"

Hudson held up two hands, but before he could apologize, the police let themselves in.

IT TOOK over an hour for the officers to sort out the trouble, take the statements, and drive Phil, Emily, and Lindsay to the station.

Taylor found herself alone with Hudson.

"I feel like I should offer to take you out for a drink, after all that drama." Hudson offered a chagrinned smile.

"You've got a few years before you can do that, I think."

He nodded. "Don't think I'll be much of a drinker, even then."

Taylor thought she might remember something about Hudson's dad drinking, but whatever the story was, it wasn't coming to mind.

"I can't believe women fall for a guy like Klaus. What kind of person jumps from woman to woman like that? I would never." Taylor ran her fingers through her hair. She felt shy all of a sudden, and also tired.

Hudson shrugged. "I don't know the guy, so I couldn't say."

"Still, I can't see myself having a messy love life like that."

"Good. It doesn't sound fun."

Hudson had hit the nail on the head; a messy love life didn't sound fun. She wanted what her parents had had. True love, faithfulness, till-death-do-you-part stuff. She couldn't imagine herself jumping from man to man or making mad decisions based on infatuation, or whatever. By the time she was Klaus and Lonnie's age, she'd have her life together, one way or the other.

"How are you feeling?" Hudson reached out as though to touch her face but stopped midway, pointing awkwardly at her nose.

"I've been better. And I can't honestly say this was all Klaus's fault."

"Sounds like there's a good story behind the black eye." He cleared his throat. "I can't offer you a drink, but we could do dinner, maybe?" Hudson had a sweet look of hope in his big eyes. He looked just like he had when she was a senior and he was a freshman, only bigger and broader. But still young and with a boyish face.

"That's sweet."

He drew his hand through his mussed-up hair. "Sweet, huh?"

"Sorry." She recognized the look of a man who felt silly. Sweet had been kind of condescending, but how old was Hudson anyway? Eighteen? Nineteen? She was a college graduate and off on her life's adventure.

"It's all good." He stuffed his hands in his pockets and ambled over to the back door.

"I'd better head out to the farm and update Grandma Quinny on how things fell into place. She'll be devastated that she missed the big showdown."

"You and your grandma are a lot alike." Hudson opened the back door.

Taylor curled her lip. "Nah, not at all. I hate this kind of drama. I only wanted to help because I found Emily. I felt sort of responsible."

"Didn't you help Isaiah at the college with a mystery thing a couple of years back?"

"That was different. He's an old friend." Taylor found her purse on the desk that was hidden by the staircase. "If I never have to be involved in something like this again, it will still be too soon."

"Never say never." Hudson held the door open for her.

"Then I'll say this: It would have to be a grave family tragedy to make me want to mess around with crime again. I'm heading off to grad school, and I'm going to wipe this entire thing from my mind."

"All of it?" he asked, his voice low and growly as she brushed past him.

"Probably." She looked up. Hudson was ridiculously good looking and sweet. But he was just too young. For now.

*A FATAL ACCIDENT. Sisters suspecting murder. Can they unravel a tangled thread of clues before the killer strikes again?*

TAYLOR QUINN HAD a good job and a cute boyfriend in the city. But when her mother dies suspiciously and she rushes home to take over the family's small-town quilt shop, her whole world unravels. Discovering her grieving young sister blames herself, she vows to prove everyone's innocence.

. . .

IN WAY OVER HER HEAD, Taylor's investigation pulls a thread of quirky suspects, a tight knot of envy, and a patchwork of gossip. But as she weaves the evidence together, she unwittingly reels in the killer's attention...

CAN Taylor sew up the case before everything comes apart at the seams?

ASSAULT AND BATTING is the first book in the delightful Taylor Quinn Quilt Shop cozy mystery series. If you like classic puzzles, poignant family relationships, and heartwarming surprises, then you'll love Tess Rothery's tangled tale.

COZY UP with your copy today!

ASSAULT AND BATTING; A Taylor Quinn Quilt Shop Mystery

AVAILABLE FOR KINDLE, in Kindle Unlimited, in paperback, large print, and audio!

# ABOUT THE AUTHOR

Tess Rothery is an avid quilter, knitter, painter, writer, and publishing teacher. She lives with her cozy little family in Washington State where the rainy days are best spent with a dog by her side, a mug of hot coffee in her hand, and something mysterious to read.

Printed by Amazon Italia Logistica S.r.l.
Torrazza Piemonte (TO), Italy

58366169R00059